Men of Action

Julie Rowe

Published by Julie Rowe, 2022.

MEN OF ACTION

First edition. March 3, 2022.

ISBN: 979-8201686796

Written by Julie Rowe.

Table of Contents

Book One

Secret Santa

***

A nurse grieving the death of her twin brother receives an unexpected gift at the staff Secret Santa party: the bullet that killed him and a message of hope and love.

***

Secret Santa

"I hate Secret Santa," Kenzie Bowman muttered to herself. She crossed her arms over her chest and leaned against the wall, as far away from the crowded hospital's emergency department lunch room table as possible. The table was covered in wrapped boxes and gift bags. A bevy of nurses rummaged through them looking for their name on a tag, squeals of glee and laughter filling the remaining space in the room.

Anyone walking by would think it was Black Friday. They'd be lucky if they didn't end up treating one of their own for a bloody nose.

She used to love Christmas. The decorations, buying just the right gift for a friend, singing carols, and spending time with the people she loved.

Until last year.

Until her twin brother, Kennon, was killed on Christmas Day.

Now, she just wanted the entire event to be over. She never wanted to see another Christmas tree, hear another Christmas song, or taste eggnog ever again.

Her friend Amy surfaced from the circling sharks with a gift in each hand. "I found yours, Kenzie," she said with Christmas cheer that darn near dripped sugar.

Oh joy.

Amy bounced up to Kenzie and thrust the gift into her hands, then proceeded to rip the paper off her own.

"Ohh," she squealed, segueing into a victory dance as she hoisted her booty into the air. "A bottle of Baileys! Santa loves me, yes he does." Amy paused mid-dance to lever her laser-sharp gaze at Kenzie. "Your turn, Ebenezer. Open it."

"What's the point? I don't wear perfume, I don't like scented candles, and I don't drink alcohol. We know the likelihood of one of those three items being in this box is eighty-six-point-three percent."

"You sound like a computer when you talk that way," Amy said, enunciating each word individually.

"Better than having your eardrums blown out by indiscriminate screaming."

Amy's eyes narrowed to two slits. "Open the box."

"Have I mentioned how much I hate Secret Santa?"

"The box, Kenzie. *Now.*"

"Fine." Kenzie rolled her eyes and picked at the festive paper. "But if this gift sucks it's going home with you."

Amy's fierce expression slowly turned into a frown. "You don't just hate Secret Santa, you hate Christmas, don't you?"

"Do you blame me?" Christmas was supposed to be a time of joy and love, spent with friends and family. All that was impossible for her now. She and Kennon had been all each other had for eight years now. A heart attack had taken Dad from them. Mom followed him to the grave four months later.

Amy glanced away at the crowd of nurses and doctors for a second, then met Kenzie's gaze. "I suppose not. But it's not healthy for you to brood." She watched Kenzie's fingers as they slowly peeled the tape from the paper. "Come to my place Christmas Day," Amy said, the words rushing out of her mouth like a five-year-old who'd had too much candy. "Don't stay home alone. Please."

"I won't be good company."

"That's why you should come."

The last of the tape came off the paper and Kenzie carefully folded it and threw it into the garbage can. The box in her hand was too small for a bottle of Baileys, so it was down to perfume or candles. She opened the top, pushed aside the tissue paper, and pulled out a glass ball about the size of her fist.

The glass was plain, no decoration or sparkles. Something hung inside it, tied up in some string. She turned the ball to see if she could get a better look—

A bullet.

A smashed, wrecked bullet.

Pain seized her diaphragm and brought her breathing to a screeching halt. The agony ricocheted through her body until even the tips of her hair hurt.

"What's that?" Amy asked, staring at the ball, confusion furrowing her forehead. "It's not very festive looking."

It could only be one thing.

"The reason why I hate Christmas." Her voice sounded strangely calm.

"Huh?"

"This isn't from staff, it's from my brother's best military buddy."

Why? Why would he do this? Give her the one thing guaranteed to rip her heart out while it was only barely still beating.

"It's the bullet that killed my brother." The words came from far, far away. Almost an echo.

Amy's gaze jerked up to meet her own. "Your brother? But I thought he... Shit," she breathed out as a whisper. "How do you know it's *that* bullet?"

"Because he tried to give it to me before."

"He *what?*"

But Kenzie wasn't listening anymore. She was drowning in sorrow. It clouded her mind, sight, and hearing, pulling her under into a dark and silent world. Somehow she walked from the lunch room to the waiting room, but she had no memory of doing it. This must be what teleportation was like. Going from location to location without the inconvenience of conventional travel.

People turned as she entered the waiting area, most of them likely hoping she'd call their name.

Except for one.

One man stood slowly, staring at her face, his gaze apologetic. He was tall and fit, with a squared face that was strong rather than handsome. Yet, every woman in the room turned to stare at him. He didn't seem to notice, his whole focus was on her.

She angled her head back sharply then turned and walked a down a hallway until she got to a large wheelchair-accessible washroom. She went inside. He followed her in and she shut and locked the door.

Kenzie glared at the man who had been trying to give her a damaged bullet for the past three months. A man she'd refused to see again after their first disastrous conversation. A man she'd told to go to hell.

A man she'd once thought she loved.

Gage Remington.

She held out the box to him. "I don't want this. I never wanted to see it and to find it in a glass ball pretending to be a Christmas ornament—" For a moment she ran completely out of breath. "Take it."

He made no effort to accept the box. "Damn it, Kenzie, he wanted you to have it."

"My brother wanted me to have the bullet that *killed* him?"

"No. He wanted you to have a reminder of what you have to live for. *We're all just a bullet or a breath away from oblivion; don't waste yours*—wasn't that the phrase you used to say goodbye with?" He took a step toward her. "He made me swear. It was the last thing he said to me before—"

She thrust a warning finger an inch from his nose. "Don't say it." She paced a step or two away, then back. "I never knew how stupid and childish it was to repeat the rhyme our grandfather taught us until the damn bullet showed up." She shoved the box at him and spun, grabbing for the door handle, but he got there before she could get the door open.

He took her shoulders into his hands and turned her.

She didn't want to see him, didn't want to touch him, didn't want to face the reality of her life with her brother—her best friend—no longer in it.

She pounded on Gage's chest and fought to get herself free.

He simply gathered her up and pulled her into his intractable embrace. Someone was crying deep, shuddering sobs that sounded like they were coming out of the throat of a tortured person.

That's when she realized—she was the person crying.

Gage whispered in her ear, "It'll be okay. I've got you now," over and over again as he rocked her. Her face was buried in his chest and his familiar scent made her cry even harder.

She'd missed him. Missed their conversations that covered every topic, conversations that often ended in argument. Missed their movie nights, when Gage and Kennon would tease her about her love of horror movies.

Kennon. She'd never get to experience any of that with her brother again.

He was dead.

Dead because he'd gotten in front of a bullet aimed at Gage.

Gage, her brother's best friend and her secret crush. All she could feel was guilt now when she looked at him. Guilt because he was alive and part of her was fiercely glad. The rest of her couldn't forgive herself for feeling that way.

So she cried.

Gage cried with her.

She wasn't sure how long the two of them wallowed in their sorrow, but it was long enough for someone to pound on the door. Amy, from the sound of the concerned voice asking if she...they were okay.

Kenzie pulled out of Gage's embrace, which was a lot harder to do than she expected, and opened the door. Tears blurred her vision and she was sure she looked like someone who'd been hit in the face with a dodge ball.

"Kenzie? Are you...all right?" Amy's wide-eyed gaze jumped between Kenzie and the tall, broad-shouldered man behind her.

"Not really." She sighed. "But when has that ever made a difference? Give me five minutes and I'll get back to work."

"No problem. I just wanted to make sure..." Amy retreated, closing the door as she went.

Kenzie stared at the door for several long seconds trying to figure out what she was going to say to the man behind her. Finally, she turned around with not an idea in her head.

Gage's eyes were bloodshot and his face as wet as hers. The front of his sweater was damp. She glanced at the mirror and discovered she looked even worse.

"Wow, we look terrible."

Gage heaved a huge sigh. "Always the realist."

"I really, *really* don't want to think about my reality right now. I have four more hours to go in my shift."

"I'm sorry." Gage said the words with a deliberation that told her he wasn't apologizing for following her into the bathroom.

"I know." She struggled to speak around the gravel in her throat. "Doesn't make it any easier, though."

"Yeah."

Kenzie grabbed a couple of paper towels from the dispenser, wet them with warm water, and cleaned up her face. "You've given me the box with the...the...thing he wanted me to have. You've said you're sorry. Are we done?"

He nodded. "For now."

"What else is there?"

"I have a story to tell you."

"A story?" She shook her head. "Gage, I'm barely holding myself together. The story is going to have to wait."

"It can," he said, his tone telling her in no uncertain terms that he wasn't giving up, he was just giving her a little time. "Ken didn't leave things to chance."

She frowned. "Are you saying he made arrangements in case he was...?"

"KIA? Yes. We all did."

"I see." She nodded. Paced. Nodded again. "All right then. I'll call you when I'm on my days off."

"Kenzie..." His voice trailed off.

"What?"

"Take care of yourself." He said it like he meant it.

She wanted to tell him that the whole idea was ludicrous, but managed to say, "I'll try."

It was the best she could do.

* * *

The ER was a place of feast or famine. Either they had more patients than chairs in the waiting room or there wasn't a soul in the place. Christmas Day was no exception, and it was standing-room only.

One of the local hotels had hosted a Christmas party the night before for three hundred people who worked for a construction company. Three-quarters of them were in the ER with all the signs of food poisoning. Hospital staff were handing out barf bags like crazy. If they had many more patients come in with severe vomiting, they were going to have to hit up an airline for more.

The adults were mostly fine. Medication to control the nausea was all most of them needed, but a few small children had been affected and they needed fluids in addition to medication. It didn't take a four-year-old long to get dehydrated when they couldn't keep anything down for twelve hours or more.

Kenzie found herself tired, fading fast, and in charge of an intravenous assembly line. So far, she'd established IVs and began pushing fluids into four kids under ten years old, two ladies in their fifties, and three men who looked like they worked outside a lot. As she finished the last one, the ER doc handed her the chart for another child—a three-year-old this time.

"You're going to need another pair of hands to hold this guy down," Dr. Barry said. "He's not a happy camper."

"Thanks." She was so tired her voice sounded like an old car motor on its last mile. "I'll see if I can find some help."

The doctor shook his head. "Good luck with that."

Kenzie went in search of another nurse, but everyone was busy with emergencies of their own.

She walked through the waiting room on her way to the small alcove where her patient and his parents waited, and spied Gage talking to one of the triage nurses. She was smiling and nodding to something he said. The nurse touched his arm in a way that told Kenzie she was very interested in sharing some "Christmas cheer" with him.

That sight sent a jagged arrow of protest through her, strong enough to have her walking toward them—to do what, she wasn't sure—but letting the other woman touch Gage as if she had every right...

Kenzie stopped cold.

She was jealous.

No, no, no, she couldn't be, but the fading anger wasn't a figment of her imagination. Guilt, so cold it cut deep into her heart, doused the anger as if it had never been. How could she be jealous of another woman's contact with Gage today of all days?

As if he'd heard her thoughts, Gage glanced up, and she found herself unable to look away. It was as if they were tied together by invisible ropes of the strongest steel. His gaze held hers for two long seconds, then he said something to the other nurse and began striding toward Kenzie like there wasn't anyone else in the room.

Kenzie actually took a half step toward him before she could stop herself. She should go—she had a patient waiting for her—but he got to her before she could leave.

"What are you doing here?" she asked.

"Looking for you."

"I'm working. Didn't I tell you that yesterday?"

"Nope. You said you'd call on your days off. I didn't realize until after I'd left that I forgot to ask when those were."

"Oh." She hadn't told him for a reason, but now that he asked she couldn't find the energy to lie. "I'm off for a couple of days when tonight's shift is over."

"Why didn't you tell me that?"

She cocked an eyebrow.

"You're not going to avoid me, Kenzie." He leaned a little closer. "I'm very good at hunting people down who try to do that."

"I believe you." She took a step back. "We're slammed right now. I might even need to work a couple of hours of overtime."

"Can I help?"

"I wish. We could use you, but I'm afraid the powers that be don't like people walking off the street and lending a hand."

"When is your shift over?"

"I've got three hours."

He nodded, gave her another hard look then moved toward the exit doors.

Kenzie watched him leave, then headed over to the triage nurse who had hit on Gage. Just the person she was looking for. "I need some help with a three-year-old."

The rest of her shift went by in a blur of taking vitals and setting up IVs. She was still doing her charting when one of the other nurses paused at the station. "There's a guy asking for you at the triage desk."

"Tall, buff, and handsome?"

"Yep."

"Thanks." She didn't look up from her charts.

"You going to keep him waiting?" The nurse sounded surprised.

"I have to finish these reports."

"He doesn't look like the patient type."

"You'd be surprised." The thing was, she didn't know why he was here, waiting for her, in the first place. He said he had a story to tell her, but that could wait. Couldn't it?

Today was not a good day for stories.

The nurse chuckled and walked away.

Ten minutes later a large shadow leaned over the desk. "Going to be long?"

Kenzie looked up into Gage's face and knew she wasn't going to be able to avoid him. "I don't know, maybe another ten or fifteen minutes."

"Can I wait here?"

She blinked. "Um, I guess." She cocked her head to one side. "Why aren't you spending today with your parents? Your sister and her kids?"

"I was with them this morning. The kids opened their gifts and we had turkey for lunch. Tonight I want to spend with a friend."

A friend. Well, what did she expect, that he would declare his undying love for her?

"I suppose I don't have a choice about that?"

He gave her a little grin. "Nope."

"Fine. Grab a seat over there." She pointed at a chair outside one of the patient cubicles a few feet away.

Gage moved with a feline grace that drew the eye of most of the staff hanging around the nursing desk, but the only person he made eye contact with was her.

For a moment she couldn't breathe. Why on earth would this tall, strong, good-looking man be hanging around waiting for her? Because of his friendship with her brother? Or was there more to it?

Ridiculous. Happy endings were for romance novels, not real life.

In real life, bad things happened to good people. Period. Any fantasies about Gage professing his love, or any other fuzzy feelings for her, were just that. Fantasies. Fiction. Stuff that was never going to happen. She'd given him hints, but he'd ignored every one.

She needed to get that through her head before the last few intact pieces of her heart got stomped on. She'd hear the man out, then get him out of her place before she could do something stupid like tell him that he starred in every one of her fantasies.

Kenzie closed the last chart, put it in the completed pile then glanced at Gage and nodded.

He followed her out of the building.

"I live about ten minutes away," she told him.

"I'll follow you."

She got into her car and drove out of the parking lot, Gage in his vehicle right behind. She parked in the lot outside her apartment and they met at the back door. She didn't talk to him until the door was closed behind him. Even then she didn't look at him, just dumped her coat on a chair and kept walking.

"Coffee?" she asked.

"Sure."

She disappeared into the kitchen.

"No Christmas decorations," he said from the living room.

"No."

He didn't say anything for a couple of seconds, then commented, "Christmas happened anyway, though."

She flinched, but managed to say in an even tone, "That it did." She poked her head around the wall separating the kitchen from the living room. "Hungry?"

"Only for conversation."

Too bad.

She smacked herself on the forehead. That was not an acceptable thought.

She brought out his coffee and a cup of tea for herself and set them on the coffee table. She sat on the couch as far away from him as she could get. It wasn't far enough. Gage was a big man—over six feet, with shoulders to match. He was also an active-duty soldier home on leave, with the muscles to prove it. He looked almost indecently sexy in the black sweater and jeans he wore.

She so wasn't going *there,* and jerked her gaze up to his face. "So...?"

"I have a story to tell you."

"Is it about Kennon?"

"Yeah."

"Am I going to want to hear it?"

"I don't know. I hope it will help, but..." He shrugged, looking oddly helpless. "He made me promise to tell you."

She sighed. "He always did think he knew best about everything."

Gage gave her a crooked smile. "Does that mean you'll listen?"

"I don't want to." A sob squeaked its way past her throat. "Why?"

"Because then I'll have to admit he's gone. And if this story is about how he died or *why* he died, I might have to give up being angry. I might have to live with the gaping black hole in my life most people call family."

Gage watched her for a moment before asking, "You're afraid?"

She gave him a thin smile that did nothing to conceal the depth of her sorrow. "I'm terrified. He wasn't just my brother; he was my twin. My earliest memory is of laughing with him while we chased a bug across the floor. He was always there for me. *Always.* But I wasn't with him when he needed me."

"I'm sorry," Gage whispered. He took her hand in his. "I really am. I wish I could go back and fix it so he didn't die, but I can't."

That simple gesture of support tore away a small piece of the dam inside her. Grief flowed out the breach, but as with all constructed things, once ruptured, the dam quickly disintegrated, releasing a year's worth of misery all at once.

The pain struck her so hard it was difficult to breathe through the sobs. Her whole body shook. She was blinded by tears and deafened by her own anguish.

Warm hands drew her forward and she encountered a hot wall of muscle covered by a soft sweater. Gage.

His arms wrapped around her, and she buried her head against his chest and cried.

* * *

There was a limit to the amount of tears a person could shed.

Kenzie wasn't sure how long she'd cried on Gage's shoulder, but her tea was cold when she finally pulled away to wipe the salty tracks off her face with a few tissues.

"Feel better?" Gage asked in a husky voice that told her he, too, had let himself grieve.

"I feel like someone stuffed this entire box of tissues up my nose."

He chuckled.

"And I have a monster headache." She winced at the damage she'd done to his sweater. "Good grief, you look like someone chucked a bucket of water on you or something."

He pulled the sweater away from his skin and examined it. "I didn't want to say anything, but it's a bit wet."

"Here, take it off. I'll wash it for you."

He looked at her with one eyebrow raised.

"I'll find you something else to wear."

"As long as it doesn't have flowers on it." He stood and pulled off the sweater, handing it to her.

She held out her hand to take it, but her gaze was stuck on the impressive musculature he'd revealed.

Gage was beautifully proportioned. Not outrageously bulked up like a bodybuilder, but nicely defined. *Very* nicely defined.

If the triage nurse had known what he looked like sans shirt, she'd have fought dirty for him.

He cleared his throat and Kenzie realized she'd been staring for far too long. "Sorry. Just wasn't expecting...um, so many..." She gave up trying to finish the sentence and offered him a weak smile. "Sorry."

"I'm not complaining."

That comment jerked her gaze back to his. He was watching her with a strange sort of smile that looked affectionate and...hungry.

No. *No.* He wasn't interested in her. He never had been before. Not when she modeled a bikini accidently on purpose, not even as a mercy date when she confessed she didn't have a date for her convocation. She was imagining things. Strange, crazy things.

She flashed him a smile, pulled the sweater to her chest, and rushed away to the closet where her washer and drier were housed.

Not running away.

Not running away.

Damn straight she was running away. If she was smart she'd keep on going, right out of the apartment and into a whole new zip code.

Gage Remington was dangerous in more ways than she could count. So dangerous, in fact, that she couldn't remember how to operate her own washing machine. Eventually she figured it out and started the sweater on a short wash cycle.

Something told her it was never going to be short enough.

She abandoned the washer for her bedroom closet in hopes of finding something large enough for Gage to wear. If she didn't find something to cover up all that male hotness she might succumb to the temptation to touch all those muscles. He didn't look inclined to stop her.

Okay, so nothing with flowers on it. She went through a pile of sweatshirts, but they were all too small. Finally, she found an old T-shirt of Kennon's that he'd left behind on a visit a couple of years before. She'd forgotten about it and finding it was a punch to the gut all over again.

But it was the only thing that would fit.

She took it out to the living room where Gage stood waiting. She stopped several feet away and held out the shirt as far as she could. He bit his bottom lip like he was having trouble stifling laughter as he took it from her.

"It was Kennon's. I found it in the back of my closet."

And just like that, the mood shifted again, into something somber and sad.

"Thanks." His voice was subdued, almost defeated.

She nodded. "I'm going to make another cup of tea. More coffee?"

"No thanks, but something hot would be good. What kind of tea are you drinking?"

"It's a green tea with some mint. Want to try it?"

"Sure."

The kettle came to a boil and she added water to her teapot. She took the pot and two mugs out to the living room and set them on the coffee table.

Gage had settled on the couch again, but seemed to take up more room than before. She poured the tea and waited for all of two seconds before her feet wanted to be off and doing something other than stay planted on the floor.

She cleared her throat. "So, the story?"

He nodded and took a deep breath. "We were out in the hills on an operation I can't tell you about, in a part of Afghanistan I can't name."

She snorted. "I was never any good at geography anyway."

"We came across a family on an old trail. There were at least three generations of them with what looked like everything they owned either on their backs or on a cart pulled by a couple of old horses. The kids got excited when they saw us and ran ahead of their parents to ask us for chocolate. I think it was one of only five words they knew in English."

He stared into space, his facial muscles moving minutely, telling her he was reliving the moment. She knew that his memory got to a rough part when his whole body jerked. "Bullets started raining down on us, creating dirt geysers all around. Two of the kids went down first. Then our lieutenant. The family was screaming and trying to hide under their wagon. Our guys were yelling, trying to find cover and figure out where the shots were coming from."

He was breathing heavily and fast, his fists clenching and unclenching on his lap.

Kenzie slid toward him and took his hands in her own.

He stopped talking for a second, swallowed hard, and held on to her with a grip that she feared would never let her go. Did she want him to let her go? No. No way. She held his hands tighter.

"I got shot in my right shoulder."

"I didn't see a scar."

"It entered from above and behind me and carved a brand-new interstate through my right lung. Hurt like a son of a bitch."

"I didn't know. Show me."

"I haven't told many people, just the family."

She waved that off and rotated her hand in a circle. "Turn around."

He twisted around and pulled the shirt up and over his shoulder. There, just above the blade, was a jagged-edged scar. She stared at it, nausea churning her stomach.

It could have easily killed him. She could have lost Kennon and Gage at the same time. She put her hand on it and traced the uneven outline of the wound with the tip of her index finger. "It looks like it was painful," she whispered.

"Yeah. It hurt, but that wasn't the worst part of it at the time." He let the shirt drop and she pulled her hand away as he turned back around. He didn't let her get far, though, grabbing her hands again and holding on.

"I was having trouble breathing—I guess my lung collapsed—and Ken was right there, covering me, returning fire, and trying to find the SOBs shooting at us."

Gage stopped talking.

Kenzie stared at him for a moment before she realized he'd stopped breathing as well. "Gage?"

"Just give me a second. I haven't told anyone this part."

She slid an inch closer. "Okay."

He took in a couple of breaths that seemed to calm him down. "One of the kids who'd been shot started to cry and move around. Ken, he ran over and grabbed the kid and plopped him down next to me. The rest of the team were trying to get themselves and everyone else out of the line of fire, but the bullets were coming in from multiple directions, so it was a losing battle.

"One of our guys started using a grenade launcher to return fire and that made a difference. I think he got a few by accident more than design. That's about when Ken got shot. The first one was in the leg. Which mostly pissed him off. He didn't move from his position covering that kid and me, just kept firing. The second one got him in the chest. The shooter must have been almost perpendicular to Ken because it got in through his armpit." Gage paused again, his hands tightening, his face pale. "Ken...went down." On the last word, Gage's voice broke and he had to take another breath before continuing. "But he fought back up to his knees and threw himself over me and the kid." Gage's composure disintegrated. He started to cry and covered his face with one hand.

She put her arms around him. The selfish part of her wanted him to stop. She didn't want to picture Kennon's death, didn't want to imagine his pain. She didn't want to put Gage through any more anguish than he was already feeling. "You don't have to finish. I can guess the rest."

He grabbed her like she was some kind of lifeline, reeled her in, held on tight, and said into her hair, "No, I have to finish. He made me promise." Gage nuzzled her neck for a few seconds, as if her scent helped to ground him, then continued. "He looked me in the eye and he said, 'Hey, asshole, I think I'm going to make it into heaven before you do.' I told him he was a greedy jerk and he laughed."

Gage stopped talking to rub his face with both hands, almost as if he was trying to rub the memory out of his mind. "Our guys were shooting, shouting, and shitting bricks." A shaky laugh escaped out of Gage's mouth, a despair-filled sound that sent a cold shiver up her back.

"Then Ken said, 'Promise me something. Survive. Go home. Give my sister the bullet in my chest. Tell her she has to hang on to it until her day comes. Whenever she's got that bullet in her hand, she's holding on to me, you got that?' I said yeah and he said, 'And tell her...'" Gage's voice died for a second then continued softly, so very softly. "'How much you love her.'"

Kenzie froze. *What?*

"A few seconds later he was dead."

She pulled back to look at Gage.

His face was blotchy with tears, yet hot with a blush. He couldn't meet her eyes.

"You..." she began, but she couldn't finish, couldn't put it into words. "Really?"

He finally met her gaze, but only for a second. "Yeah."

This big, strong, attractive guy who could have his pick of women loved her?

"No. That can't be true." How could he have hidden it from her for years? "You're lying."

He looked her in the eye again and didn't drop the contact. "Why would I lie about that?"

"Guilt."

He shook his head. "I feel guilt, but not because of my feelings for you. That might have been the reason if you'd been Ken's wife, but you're his sister."

"Oh." She stared and tried to understand, but it didn't make sense. "If that's how you feel why didn't you tell me this before?"

"You're his sister."

She blinked. "Now I'm confused."

"You'd already lost him to the military and I saw how much you missed him. Then to have a boyfriend in the same situation? I couldn't do that to you. He would have killed me for making you hurt that way." He shook his head with finality. "A man doesn't mess with his best friend's sister."

"What, there are rules?"

"Unwritten, unspoken, undeniable rules," he said with a voice harder than stone.

"That's ridiculous."

"Are you saying women don't have rules about poaching another woman's man or dating a friend's ex?"

"We definitely do have rules for that, but I didn't realize men did. I mean, I know about the 'bros before hos' rule—"

"Completely fabricated by Hollywood."

"Whatever. I just didn't know there were more."

"You're avoiding the subject."

"I...he...you." She blew out a frustrated gust of air. "Men."

Gage stared at her with a small smile. "You're blushing."

He wasn't supposed to notice. "I am *not.*"

"A gentleman would let you get away with it."

She waited all of two seconds before asking, "Are you a gentleman?"

"Nope. I most definitely am not." He tilted her chin up so she had to meet his gaze. "I'm not letting you off the hook."

She tried to pull away, put some distance between them, but he held her with arms that refused to budge.

"No running away, either," he said, brushing a kiss into her hair.

That quick touch was enough to make her shake. She had yet to come to grips with her brother's death and Gage expected her to take his declaration calmly?

"I don't know if I can handle all this." She sniffed, but instead of giving her some space, he shifted on the couch, reclining a little and pulling her so she rested on his torso, her head snuggled under his chin.

"No need to fuss."

"Fuss?" Such an old-fashioned word.

"I should have told you how I felt ages ago. Ken used to yank my chain regularly about it."

"I don't know what to say." She'd always been attracted to Gage, always wished for more between them, but his friendship with her brother made that secret fantasy impossible. That polite barrier between them had darn near killed her. He only told her now because Kennon made him promise. He probably wouldn't have told her at all if he hadn't been forced into it. Would he come to regret their relationship?

"Don't say anything then."

"But—"

"I didn't tell you so you'd feel bad. I told you because I said I would. *You* don't have to do anything."

"So, you just tell me something you've been keeping to yourself for five years, and I'm just supposed to smile and carry on as if you hadn't said anything?"

"If that's what you want to do, yep."

Was that what she wanted to do? She let herself relax, soaking up his body heat, and for the first time in a long time discovered she felt safe. Whole. Sad, but not immersed in the soul-wrecking pain she'd endured for all the long months since she'd been notified of Kennon's death.

"When I found out Kennon was dead," she said to Gage's shirt. "That he died protecting you—because they told me that much—I was angry."

He rubbed her back in reply.

"I blamed you and I piled all my rage and grief on you."

"Yeah, I figured that's what happened."

"That damned bullet was the *last* thing I ever wanted to see, but..."

"But?"

"Kennon was never one for doing things like anyone else. Why should his death be any different? You were right to give it to me." Her voice fractured on the last word.

"I'm sorry it hurt you so much to see it."

"I think I needed to hurt. I got stuck at the angry stage of grief and didn't know how to get myself out of it, then you came along and knocked me out of my rut."

"That's me, a rut knocker outer."

Alarm bells went off in her head. He was trying to be funny. Trying much too hard. "I thought you weren't going to let me off the hook?"

A subtle tension entered the muscles under her. "Oops."

She lifted her head so she could look him in the eyes. "Well?"

He shrugged. "You're not trying to beat me up, or kill me, so I figure you're doing okay."

She examined his face for deceit and found none, but his tense shoulders told her he was nervous about something. He still had his arms around her, but they were oh so carefully placed. Too carefully.

The entire situation her brother had managed to place both her and Gage in suddenly became clear.

"Kennon never told you, did he?"

"Told me what?"

"That rat." The day she'd discovered her brother reading her diary, he'd teased her without mercy. Reading her most private feelings out loud while she chased him around the room, he'd laughed so hard. She'd been sure he was going to give Gage a few hints.

"Excuse me?" Gage asked.

"That sneaky, underhanded *rat*." She sat up, pulled out of Gage's arms, and stood next to him with her hands on her hips. "He is without a doubt sitting in heaven laughing his ass off at both of us."

Gage stared at her like she'd lost her mind.

She held out her hand to him. "Come with me."

"Where?"

"Just come."

He took her hand and stood. She towed him out of the living room and down the short hallway to her bedroom.

* * *

She flipped on the light, let go of Gage's hand, and went to her dresser to rummage through a drawer.

"I'll just wait out here." Gage pointed at the hallway and began to move away.

"Oh no you don't," she said, grabbing him again and pulling him inside. Kenzie pushed him to sit on the end of the bed. "Stay right there. I want to show you something."

He let out a grunt that sounded frustrated and a little mad. "I'd like to show you something too, but I doubt we're talking about the same thing."

She froze, then turned her head to stare at him. Did he just say what she thought he did?

He rubbed his hands against his jeans-clad thighs. "Sorry."

"No you're not."

He glared at her. "This is not a good idea."

"What isn't?"

"You and me. In your bedroom. Together."

"Nervous?"

The look he gave her could have started a forest fire in the middle of a hard rain. "If you knew what I was thinking you'd be nervous too."

"If I know anything at all, it's that I'm safe with you."

A combination of resolve and despair flowed over his face. It finally solidified into determination and he nodded. "You got me there."

She turned her attention back to the drawer, found the item she was looking for, and hauled it out. Her journal.

She opened it and flipped through the pages. "Here we go." She turned the book around and held it out to Gage. "Read this."

"What is it, your diary or something?"

"Sort of. I wrote all kinds of stuff in there. Dreams, poetry, goals. I stopped writing in it when Kennon died." Gage stared at her with a frown on his face. "Come on, read."

He finally looked at the book in his hands. "The date says three years ago."

She stood in front of him with her hands propped on her hips. "Yeah, and?"

"Bossy," he mumbled as he read. He didn't rush, so she knew when he got to the part she wanted him to see when he suddenly straightened out of his slouch. His gaze jerked up to meet hers.

"Keep reading."

He closed the book and set it carefully onto the floor.

"What are you—" Her voice died as he got to his feet, his eyes going from wide to narrow.

"It says you love me."

"I know what it says. I wrote it."

He took a step forward. "Still feel that way?"

She took a step back, her gaze dancing over his body. "Yes, but you need to see the rest of what I wrote." He stood tall, leaning toward her, his hands reached out to take her by the shoulders and halt her retreat.

He grinned, a slow, sensual slide upward of his lips that told her making him read about her feelings for him in her bedroom might not have been the smartest thing to do.

Or maybe it was exactly right.

"I'll read it later. After I kiss you." He brought her closer, then paused for a brief moment. "You okay with that?" Even as he asked he was gathering her close, one hand behind her back, the other tangled in her hair, cradling her head.

She'd never been this close, never guessed how good he'd smell, how dwarfed she'd feel in his arms. But instead of that being a bad thing, it was good. She could give someone else control. Give him everything she was, and he'd take exquisite care of it. Of her.

His head came down.

He was going to...

His lips grazed her cheek, her ear. He nipped at the lobe and sucked it into his mouth.

Her eyes slid shut at the pleasure his touch set ablaze inside her.

"Okay?" he asked again.

"What?" Her hands slid around his torso and she lifted herself into his body. Why was he talking? They had more important things to do right now. "Yes, yes."

His mouth came down on hers, his tongue swiping across her bottom lip in a tantalizing tease. She chased it, sucking on it, inviting him to taste her. He didn't hesitate, took what she offered and returned the favor with interest.

So good. His kiss was addicting and delicious. His lips never stopped sipping from her, never stopped taking her into another place where time didn't matter. Only the drugging pleasure his kiss fed into her system.

A large, hot hand cupped her breast and she moaned at the sensation. He molded and squeezed her tender flesh, his fingernail flicking across her nipple, and she jerked in reaction, the jolt of pleasure so acute it shocked her.

She wanted more. She wanted them both naked so she could feel his skin against hers. She'd probably die from pleasure overload, but she didn't care.

She'd denied herself the comfort of other people for so long her body would not be denied any longer.

Her hands groped at the shirt she'd loaned him, shoving it up and out of the way so she could run her hands over his chest. His muscles felt even better than they looked—solid and hard, covered by smooth, soft skin.

Her fingers went to the button on his jeans, then the zipper. She couldn't wait to get her hands on...

"Whoa, slow down." Gage might be out of breath, but he was fast enough to catch her hands with his.

"Party pooper."

He chuckled. "We're not on a time limit, are we?"

"No." It had been so long since she'd felt anything but grief that her pleasure-starved body was greedy for every touch, kiss, and caress. He kissed her, then kissed her again. His breathing jagged. "Damn, but I don't want to stop."

Yes. "So don't."

He laughed and stopped kissing her to rest his forehead against hers. "You're a hard woman to resist, Kenzie, but we need to talk a bit more before we do anything else. Because I have a feeling the next thing we do will be on that bed right there with us naked."

She was all for that. "Okay."

"Good." He let out a breath. "You love me?"

"Yes. I have for years."

He let her hands go and stroked her face. "I love you too. Have from the first day I met you."

That long? "I had no idea."

"Well, being Ken's sister meant I had to keep it to myself." He rubbed a thumb over her bottom lip and said, "I remember the first time I saw you. You walked into the room, just home from the gym, and you were sweaty, but all I saw was this gorgeous gal, who damn near glowed and made every cell in my body come to attention. You talked about your job and how you felt it was a calling. A call to service, and

I thought, *wow, here's my perfect woman.* Ken took one look at my face and he knew. Told me if I ever touched you, he'd cut my hands off."

"He didn't."

"He did. He took it back a couple of years later, but by then I'd already decided not to tell you. Ken found a way to change my mind, though."

Her brother's name doused her in ice water. "Maybe we shouldn't... I mean—"

"Now, darlin', he's been gone for a year. There's no shame in enjoying what we have together. It's what he wanted."

"I still feel guilty."

He held her a little tighter. "Me too."

Kennon had been gone for a year, and today was Christmas. Maybe it was time she started letting go of her anger and grief. "This all seems like a dream. You really love me?"

His voice rumbled inside his chest. "Yep. I've spent some long, lonely nights thinking about what it would be like to kiss you, touch you."

"Don't think. Let's do."

"I don't want this to be a casual thing, Kenzie. I want all of you."

"What does that mean?"

"An exclusive relationship. You and me. I want to find out if you talk in your sleep and what you look like in the morning after a night of making love." He caressed her hair and face, his fingers lingering on her skin. "I want to find out what brings you the greatest pleasure."

"Are you asking me to...marry you?"

"That's on my list, but I was going to wait a few months yet."

Oh, wow. The idea was a wonderful kind of scary, but one she was sure Kennon would have loved. His sister and his best friend together. "Okay, okay. I can deal with that."

"Yeah?"

"Yeah."

He put a hand under her chin and tilted her head up. "Be sure, because once we get started, I'm not sure I can stop."

The hand cradling her face trembled. Was it possible that she brought this fierce, tough man to a place where he felt that strongly? He'd made himself vulnerable to her. Could she do any less for him?

"I'm sure," she said, covering his hand with hers. "I'm absolutely positive."

He groaned and kissed her.

She kissed him back, her hands rising to slide around him and hold on tight. She had no intention of ever letting him go.

He picked her up, startling a squeak out of her, and laughed as he carried her the few feet to the bed. He followed her down, covering her body with his, one knee between her thighs, and she gloried in his weight.

His hands explored her body with a frenzy that inspired her own sort of crazy.

"Clothes off," she panted, tugging at the shirt he wore, tearing at his jeans.

He pulled her scrub shirt up and over her head. It disappeared somewhere south of the bed. Gage's gaze dropped to her breasts and stayed. "Wow."

She glanced down at her bra, a lacy confection that had cost her a pretty penny. "I wore this to cheer myself up."

He grinned. "Well, it works for me."

She laughed. "You're such a guy."

His hands went around her back and he unhooked her bra, then slid it slowly down her arms.

The bra went south too.

His gaze was hot enough to make her perspire, but when he touched her, cupping both breasts, she darn near set off the fire alarm. His touch was a live wire to her system, lighting her up and setting her off on an exploration of her own.

She attacked his jeans. At least, she tried to. His overwhelming interest in her breasts pulled her astray and into a state where pleasure was all she knew.

"God, you're so responsive," he whispered.

Good Lord, she'd been moaning ever since he got her bra off. "And you're a tease."

"Well, I can't have you saying that." He kissed her again as he coaxed her to lift her hips so he could tug her scrub pants off.

He took one look at her panties, groaned, and rested his head on her belly.

"Gage? What's wrong?" She looked down to find what she expected, the panties to match the bra.

"Not a damn thing," he said, looking at her. "Your underwear just short-circuited my brain."

"So shut it off. You don't need it right now anyway."

"Truer words have never been spoken." He shucked his jeans and underwear, then donned the condom she handed him from her bedside table drawer. He rejoined her on the bed, kissing her as he covered her and took her in his arms.

His strong, muscular lines fit her curves like he'd been made for her and she found herself crying as he joined his body with hers.

"You okay, darlin'?" His voice was a rumble in her ear.

"Yes," she replied, laughing and crying at the same time. "I'm just a little overwhelmed."

He nuzzled her cheek. "We have all the time in the world."

"But I want..." She had to catch her breath. "I want you to..."

He kissed her again. "I know, and I'm yours."

"I'm yours."

Gage made love to her then and for a long time, it was Kenzie who didn't think at all.

Kenzie woke to a rumbling stomach and a man curled around her like a cat. She rolled to look at him and found him watching her with a smile. "Morning."

"Hi." She stroked her hand over his chest. "I was half-afraid that yesterday was a dream."

"Nope. All real." He pursed his lips. "What was it you wanted me to read in your journal?"

Her face heated, but she didn't drop his gaze. "I wanted you to see the exact moment I fell in love with you. It was only the second time we saw each other, but you'd helped our neighbor, Mrs. Russell, bring in her groceries after she broke her arm. I don't think you knew anyone saw you, but you were so kind and polite, and so damn hot, I just couldn't keep my eyes off you."

He grinned and kissed her quick. "Get up. I have a gift for you." He climbed out of bed like a sleek panther and picked up his jeans. From the pocket, he pulled out a velvet bag and handed it to her.

Kenzie opened the bag and pulled out a charm bracelet with three gem-colored charms on it. One diamond clear and two emerald green. "Our birth months?"

He nodded. "Do you like it? Is it okay?"

"It's lovely." She tilted her head to one side. "But you already gave me the best gift ever."

"I have?"

"You."

"That gift wasn't from me. It was from Ken. He's the one who sent me here."

Joy at the happiness of their future together and sadness from the grief of losing her twin combined to rain tears down her face. "My Secret Santa."

"Mine too," Gage said, turning onto his back and drawing her across his chest. "Mine too."

Epilogue

One year later...

"Are you ready?" Amy's voice was breathless and high with excitement.

Kenzie stared at herself in the full length mirror then cleared her throat. "No, but that's never stopped me before." She'd always been strong, willing to take risks because she had always had the unswerving support of her twin. But Kennon was dead. Killed in action. This next step into her new life, she had to do alone.

She smoothed her hands down her dress and picked up the bouquet of flowers. "Let's get this show on the road." Composed of white and pink roses with a tail of snap dragons of the same colors, it gave her hands something to do other than shake.

Perhaps not completely alone. Around her neck was a white gold chain. Dangling from it was a smashed bullet. A bullet her brother had insisted she keep with her. The bullet that took her brother's life, but brought her and Gage together.

"You look gorgeous," Amy told her with a naughty grin. "Gage is going to want to throw you over his shoulder, carry you off and ravish you in the first room he can find with a lock on the door."

"I feel like I'm going to fly apart," Kenzie confessed in a hushed voice. "I don't know what's wrong with me."

"Getting married is a big deal, hon."

Kenzie gave Amy a sour look. "That's not helping."

"I know what will, seeing your man waiting for you at the altar." Amy went to the door, opened it and slipped out. A moment later she returned with a tall man in a military dress uniform.

Gage's father, Michael.

Gage's family had accepted her as if she'd been their own all along. This Christmas, the huge hole in her heart where her own parents had once resided, was now filled with the family her amazing man brought with him.

Michael smiled at her and offered her his arm. "Ready?"

She looked at the older version of the man she was about to marry and the anxiety left her in a rush that made her giddy. "Yes."

She took his arm, and he led her to the doors leading into the church proper. Amy went first, then after a count of six seconds, she and Michael went through the door.

This wasn't a full military wedding, no arch of swords. Kenzie had wanted it to stay simple, so it was just close family and friends in attendance. Everyone disappeared as soon as she met Gage's gaze. It didn't matter that they were across the church from each other, she felt their connection zip through her from the tips of her toes to the ends of her hair.

She didn't remember walking up the aisle.

The next thing she knew, Michael was handing her over to Gage with a few quiet words, to which Gage answered, "Yes, sir."

He took her hand and they turned to the priest who smiled at both of them and began speaking. The words were all the traditional ones, and Kenzie found it difficult to pay attention to him when all she wanted was to soak in Gage's smile and the love in his eyes.

Suddenly, they were at the vows and she had to yank her attention back to the priest who repeated the words she was to say.

Love.

Honor.

Cherish.

From this day forth.

Man and wife.

They slipped the rings on each other's fingers, then Gage was kissing her.

She was now Mrs. Gage Remington.

She was *married*.

Her stomach felt like someone had poured an entire bottle of champagne into it direct. The two of them looked at each other after the kiss was over with identical shocked expressions on their faces. *Yep, it was a done deal.*

They laughed, and then they were running down the aisle toward the car waiting for them. She got her dress into the passenger seat somehow, while Gage got in the driver's seat. They peeled out of the parking lot like their vehicle was a dragster.

"What's the rush?" she asked, laughing. She was married, *married*, to Gage.

"We've got a little detour to take."

"What?" Not to their reception? She took a good look at his face and narrowed her gaze at the smile flirting with her on his lips. "Where are you taking me?"

"You'll see."

The sneak.

Fifteen minutes later, Gage parked the car in the lot of the VA hospital.

Kenzie stared at the building, her chest tight, then at her husband. "Why here?" Sadness pulled some of the joy out of her voice.

Gage took her hands in his and leaned toward her. "There are a couple of guys who wanted to meet you, but they're both patients."

He wasn't making sense. "They wanted to meet me on our wedding day?"

"I wanted you to meet them on our wedding day," he said, giving her hands a squeeze. "They were with Ken and I when he died."

"Oh." The champagne party in her stomach went flat. Yet, this must be important to him or he wouldn't have brought her here.

Gage kissed the backs of her hands then held them to his lips for a moment. "They're happy for us, Kenzie, and I think Ken would approve of letting them give their blessing, too."

Her family's blessing was the one thing she was missing. Damn it, she wasn't going to cry, she *wasn't.* "You know me so well." She could almost hear Ken saying, *"Suck it up princess."* "Okay." She sucked in a deep breath and nodded. "Let's do it."

They went inside and she found herself accepting congratulations from everyone they passed. By the time they arrived at a large room where several people were playing games or watching TV, she was blushing from head to toe.

Everyone in the room was bandaged up, and several were missing limbs.

Two men playing cards caught sight of Gage and Kenzie in the entranceway and let out a whoop. "It's the bride and groom."

The room erupted in applause and Gage brought Kenzie over to meet the two men.

"This is Tom Scholtz and Barry Franklin," Gage told her with a note of pride in his voice. Then he cleared his throat, and Kenzie realized her new husband was on the verge of tears. "Gentlemen, this is Kennon's sister and my wife, Kenzie."

These men *mattered* to him.

She ignored the stares and continued wishes of congratulations from the people around them to take her lover's face in her hands and kiss him like they were utterly alone.

Until someone cleared their throat. Loudly.

She smiled at the rueful expression on Gage's face, *why had they come here again?* and turned.

"Great to meet you, ma'am," Tom said to her, extending his left hand rather than his right. His right hand and forearm were missing.

"I'm glad to meet you too," she said and realized in a rush that she was glad, incredibly glad to meet both men. They'd been Ken's brothers, men he'd served with and chosen as friends.

"Kennon told us hundreds of stories of the shit you two got into," Barry said, offering his right hand. He was missing his left leg, but used a prosthetic one that he seemed comfortable with.

"Lies, all lies," she replied with a grin and a wink.

"That's just what Ken said you'd say," Tom laughed.

She and Gage visited for a while, so grateful for the chance to talk to Tom and Barry about Ken and listen to their stories. It wasn't long however before the two men chased them off, saying, "Go on, you've got a party to get to."

"We'll be back," she promised them.

"Good," Tom said.

They got back into the car and as they drove out of the parking lot, she put her hand on Gage's thigh. "How did you know I needed that?" Needed to know Ken's friends from the military, needed another connection to the brother she'd lost. It was a part of his life she hadn't shared with him, but now she was getting to know her brother as a man, and not just her twin.

"You're a lot like Kennon. He had a lot of friends because he gave a shit. They all knew how important you were to him." Gage picked up her hand and kissed her palm. "And I know how important he was to you."

Happy tears ran down her face. "I love you."

They didn't say anything else until Gage parked the car at the hotel where the reception was taking place.

"Ready?" he asked.

"More than ready." She smiled and kissed him.

"I love you," he said as he kissed her again. And again. "Are you sure we have to show up for this dinner? Couldn't we go straight to the honeymoon suite?" he asked, nuzzling her neck.

"Nope," she said, throwing her door open and sliding out of the car. "Last one to the reception has to wash dishes for a year," she shouted as she ran for the entrance.

Gage chased after her. "Not if I catch you first!"

Kenzie dashed into the hotel, laughing, knowing this was just the beginning of a new life.

Book Two
A Pirate's Vacation

* * *

A year ago, Emergency Room doctor Josie Zizzo lost her husband to the violence in war-torn Syria. Watching him die while bullets rained down on their makeshift hospital, left her suffering from Post-Traumatic Stress disorder. Returning to work in the ER proved impossible, the PTSD throwing her back in time to the awful day her husband died. In an effort to heal, Josie buys a B&B in the U.S. Virgin Islands, but the property needs more repairs than she anticipated. Her best friend promises to come help, but it's her best friend's brother who steps off the plane, firefighter Mark Durant. Mark is the last man she dated before meeting her husband, a man she loved, a man who walked away from her when she asked for more than a causal relationship.

Mark has come to help Josie because he's suffering his own PTSD nightmare and hopes the sun, sand and time spent with the most giving woman he's ever met will help him heal. It isn't until he steps off the plane and sees Josie's shocked face that he realizes his sister has set them both up. Now he's sharing a house with a woman he wants more than his next breath, who's also fighting her own terrifying memories. It isn't until a storm hits the island that they're forced to face their pasts and all the ghosts that haunt them. Can love survive nature's wrath and their personal demons?

* * *

A Pirate's Vacation

It was a good day to be a pirate.

Not a cloud in the sky, the winds were fair and from the east. The late-morning heat was enough to put even the most athletically inclined person into a doze. The perfect time to land on the sand and hunt down some treasure—or in this case, fix it up, make it all shiny, and hope the tourists showed up.

At least, that's what Josie Zizzo hoped.

Then again, nothing had gone the way she'd hoped for the past year.

Oh, who was she kidding? Her life had virtually ended when her husband died in front of her eyes.

Both of them were emergency-room physicians, though at different Boston hospitals. They'd signed on to a medical mercy mission in Syria. One week into the mission, their makeshift hospital had come under fire by two different groups. Her husband, Adler, had been hit in the chest. Unable to move because of constant gunfire, she'd watched, every second a stab to her gut, a slash to her heart, as he bled out.

It had taken her a week to get home to Boston with her husband's body. Another week before his service and burial, then twelve weeks to realize she'd never be able to go back to life as she knew it again.

Her first shift back in the ER had made her new reality clear. The noise, the people, the blood—suddenly she was back in Syria watching Adler die. Again.

She'd screamed herself hoarse.

Again.

Post-traumatic stress disorder, they'd said. She needed therapy, time, and probably a different job, for a while at least.

So she'd left the hospital and began searching for something completely different from her Boston home. It took her six months to figure out what she wanted, but she finally decided on an entirely new way of life.

A bed-and-breakfast. The Caribbean. Pirates.

Of all the dreams she and Adler had together, running a B&B on an island that had once been home to convicts, rum runners, and the infamous pirates wasn't one of them.

She bought the first property that had appeared feasible. Something that needed fixing to make it nice. So when she arrived on the island of St. Thomas six weeks ago to take possession of her new home it had been with the hopes of getting the place ready for her first guests within a month.

That time frame had been unceremoniously dashed against the rocks. The Pirate's Cay, as her B&B was known to the locals, had needed a lot more repairs than she realized from the report and pictures the real-estate agent had sent her, but because the home had sold for a lot less than fair market value, she really couldn't complain too much.

The price had been too good to be true.

Fool's gold.

No treasure here.

Thankfully, she'd called on her best friend, Benita Durant, to come to the island to help her out for a few weeks. Benita had been her rock after she'd gotten back to Boston from Syria. Helped with the service and burial arrangements. Encouraged her to move to the Caribbean, saying the sunshine, heat, and slower lifestyle were just what the doctor ordered.

Between the two of them, they could get it all done.

Hopefully.

Possibly.

Maybe.

All Benita had to do was get off the plane and pick up her luggage, then they could get to work on making The Pirate's Cay the island's hidden gem.

Yeah, keep telling yourself that, Josie. You're just putting off the inevitable mental meltdown.

So here she was, at the airport stretched up onto her tiptoes, looking for Benita's brown ponytail among the passengers exiting the luggage carousel area.

So far, no Benita.

A group of laughing vacationers from somewhere cold—given their lack of tans—blocked her view for a couple of minutes. When they cleared out of the way, Benita wasn't in sight, but her brother was.

The sight of him kicked Josie in the diaphragm like a bad-tempered mule.

Mark Durant stood six foot two and had shoulders to match his height. Built like a football linebacker, he didn't need to tackle Josie to push her over. A puff of wind would have done the job. Mark was the last man she expected to see.

The last man she'd dated before meeting Adler.

A man she had wanted with every breath in her body, but walked away from because she wanted what he couldn't give her. A marriage. A home. A family.

A man who'd told her in no uncertain terms he wasn't ready to settle down.

"Hey," he said, staring at her with a gaze that never wavered and a smile that bordered on sinful. His voice flowed over her like dark chocolate, heady and rich.

She swallowed around a lump the size of Manhattan to say, "Hi." It came out like a croak.

He stared at her while she tried to process the fact that her best friend, whom she'd talked to only yesterday, had set her up.

Mark's expression slowly morphed into a frown. Then it dove into surprise. "Holy shit, you were expecting Benita."

"Yup," Josie said. She tried for a weak smile, but highly doubted it looked happy at all.

Mark, who had his duffel bag slung over his shoulder, dropped the bag on the floor. He shoved his hands in his jean pockets. "She told me you needed... She showed me pictures and an email you'd written asking for..." His voice trailed off and his gaze dropped to his bag.

"Help?" Josie finished for him.

He glanced at her with sad eyes and a grin curving his lips, and she caught her breath at the impact of his expression. "Yeah."

He had the best puppy-dog eyes of any man she'd ever met. Hands down, bar none.

Years disappeared and it felt like yesterday when he'd last kissed her, put his hands on her body, and made love to her. It weakened her knees and turned her breathing into something totally optional.

Well, wasn't this just ducky. Hell of a time for her libido to come out of hibernation.

Josie sighed, put some starch in her legs, and refused to succumb to the seduction of her memories. She would be polite and friendly, that was all. "Come on, you're here. You might as well get the nickel tour."

He didn't move. "Not necessary. I can grab the first plane going back to mainland USA."

That duffel bag was full. He hadn't planned a short trip.

She raised one eyebrow. "Did you take time off to come here?"

He froze like she'd just caught him with his hand in the cookie jar. "Um, yeah."

Shit. "How long?"

"Four weeks."

That rocked her back on her feet.

"From the pictures, I can tell your new place needs a lot of work."

Heh, she should have asked his opinion before she bought it. And he'd come all this way to help her, despite knowing the status of the B&B.

"What made you decide to help me?" She tried that smile thing again; maybe this time it'd work. "I mean, we haven't seen each other in a few years."

"Five."

"I beg your pardon?"

"We haven't seen each other in *five* years."

He kept track?

"Like I said," he continued. "I saw the photos of the place you bought and knew you'd need help. When Benita said you asked her to come down and give you a hand, well, I said I was handier." He shrugged. "I'm pretty good with electrical stuff and not bad with plumbing. But you weren't expecting me and you sure as hell...heck...didn't seem happy to see me just now, so—"

She tilted her head to one side. "You're already here and my main backup generator isn't working. After that, I have all the problems you mentioned. Electrical, plumbing, a leaky roof, some carpentry, and a lot of landscaping that needs to be done. Think you could handle a working man's holiday?"

"Can you?"

That was the question.

Could she do it without him? Yes, but it would take a lot longer, cost more.

He was an old friend who wanted to help, that's all.

Yeah, keep telling yourself that, Josie.

"Yup. Let's go." She turned to lead the way to her tiny, ancient Japanese car, catching just the beginning of a smile crossing his face as he picked up his bag to follow her.

What the hell had Benita told him?

The drive from the airport took only fifteen minutes. The B&B was located up the hill, with a fantastic view of the harbor. The building itself wasn't new, which was part of the problem. It needed a new roof and some of the siding needed to be replaced. Probably damage done during the last hurricane to hit the island. Aside from the view, the property did have other high points. Built into the slope, the house had three main living levels with six bedrooms, each with an ensuite bathroom, scattered throughout. There was a beautiful terrace, overlooking a pool located one level down, and a kitchen a chef would kill for.

She parked her car behind the house in front of the small garage, which was full of tiles for the roof, planks, a table saw, tools, and a whole lot of junk.

"I'm sorry things aren't as..." Her voice trailed off as she tried to imagine how it all appeared to Mark. The plants and landscaping had taken over the yard like they'd won the roundup and the cowboys had been evicted. She winced. "I haven't got much of a green thumb."

He shrugged. "Cleaning up the landscaping won't take long, a day or two. It's the roof we want to tackle first."

"The backup generator is at the top of my priority list, too." She took in a deep breath. "Okay, let's get your stuff in a bedroom so you can see the rest of the place."

He wasn't content to take a quick inspection—he knocked on the walls, inspected the ceilings, and stamped on the floors. They went through every room, all around the outside and circled the perimeter of the property.

"This is fantastic," he said, as they stood on the terrace, the ocean stretching out from the edges of the island to the horizon.

She blinked. The list of things to do was a long one. She should know, she'd written it. "Fantastic?"

He turned to her with an excited grin. "You're right, that was the wrong word. This is *awesome*. You can really do something with this place. Whatever you want."

She stared at him and said, "What have you been smoking?"

He laughed and punched her on the shoulder, which nearly knocked her to the ground. "Oops," he said, grabbing her around the waist and hauling her up against him.

Her hands landed on his chest, the muscles there hard and hot enough to scald. His scent teased her nose, drawing her in, making her want to taste. Strong arms held her close and her gaze rose to lock with eyes the color of the Caribbean Sea.

Adler's eyes had been brown.

Ice, cold and sharp, stabbed deep into her chest and she reared back.

Mark kept hold of her shoulders, but set her carefully away a couple of steps, his voice a soothing balm on her wounds. "Sorry, didn't mean to knock you over."

Pulse pounding in her ears, breathing rapid and rough, she struggled to pull her frayed nerves together with little more than ghostly cobwebs of a woman who hadn't existed in a year. "I'm o-okay." It came out in a stutter.

He winced. "Really?"

She stared at him, the concern on his face turning his eyes and mouth sad. The invisible gash in her chest grew, the ice spidering out, making her arms and hands shake. "No." The word slipped through her lips. She really hadn't meant to say it, especially to this man, who'd come thousands of miles to help her.

"Hey," he said softly, drawing her toward him. "Hey, it's all right." His arms came around her. "It's okay for you to lean on a friend." One large hand cradled her head against his chest.

Through her tears she asked, "Are you my friend?"

His voice rumbled beneath her ear. "Yes."

She'd been so alone since Adler died—alone, adrift, and rudderless. No safe harbor. Could she trust a man who'd already broken her heart once?

She wrapped her arms around him and held on.

Minutes, or hours, later her tears finally dried up and she backed out of Mark's embrace. "Thanks for letting me get you all wet."

He glanced at his shirt and chuckled. "No problem. I'm not scared of a little saltwater."

"A useful quality, especially here."

He moved away to examine the roof. "Have you had any storms since you arrived?"

Giving her a chance to pull herself together?

"A few rain showers, but no high winds." She wiped her face with the hem of her T-shirt.

He stared at it for another moment. "Roof or generator, which first?" When he transferred his gaze to her face, she realized he was waiting for her to answer.

"Roof. I've got all the supplies and I'm ready to go on it."

"Good."

"But first," Josie said, trying to follow Mark's lead and keep things casual. "Burgers and beer."

"Jo," he said with a huge grin. "You're talking my language."

***

It took them four days to finish the roof. Mark had spent the most time up there, but only after Josie had insisted on slathering him with sunblock.

Pure torture.

His muscles were taut and hard, yet supple. Her hands shook the first time she put the lotion on his naked back, but he never said a word. Her hands didn't shake the next day, but the rest of her did.

She'd forgotten how seductive stroking a man's body could be. How addicting. Warm skin over firm muscles drew her in, teasing her intimacy-starved body until it was all she could do to let him begin work every morning. Her body wasn't the only part of her starving for the comfort of a man. Her bruised and battered heart needed care and concern, and he provided it with effortless generosity.

He was familiar, a friend.

He'd also run from her five years ago when she'd wanted more than a physical relationship, and torn her heart out in the process.

Had he changed?

Had *she* changed?

The questions circling her brain were driving her crazy.

Luckily for her the roof was done, so her major temptation was more out of sight. Mark had moved on to repair the generator located in the lowest floor of the building. Not exactly a storm cellar, but also not a living space, either. The only thing she was certain of was that it was the oldest part of the house with heavy beams composing the walls and ceiling. The beams were dark, as if stained with pitch or oil. Between the beams was a primitive sort of cement made of local sand and crushed shells, or so the real-estate agent claimed.

The generator, which was large and heavy, had to be connected to the home's wiring manually and was used only if the solar power panels on one section of the roof were damaged or covered.

It hadn't been used in a year or two.

Mark had examined it, taking it apart before deciding he needed a few parts. He'd taken off to check a couple of shops that sold parts, electronics, and certified junk.

She'd decided to tackle some of the siding and even managed to replace a couple of planks before Mark returned, excited with his finds in town.

"I think I got this licked," he said to her. He held out some spark plugs, a wire brush, and some kind of cleaning oil. His smile was reminiscent of a little boy who'd discovered tadpoles in a pond and had scooped up a pail of them.

"You mean, the problem is...it's dirty?"

"I don't think that thing has been cleaned and the plugs changed since it was new."

"Wow, I hope it's that simple."

"I checked out some of the plumbing problems you're having in the upstairs bathrooms," he said, as if they'd done this a million times. He took the wire brush coated with a little cleaning oil to the spark plug connections on the generator. "Again, I think they're fairly simple fixes. A couple of upgrades on some of the pipes, especially the elbows, to copper. Right now some of it's copper and some is brass, and that is where the problems start."

"Will it be expensive to buy the new pipes?"

"It'll be a few bucks—copper isn't cheap—but you don't need too much of it, either, so..."

"Okay, okay." She walked the length of the tiny room and back again.

Mark watched her for a moment then went back to cleaning the generator. "What's going on in that head of yours?"

"What do you mean?"

"You're pacing." He glanced at her as he worked. "You've been a big ball of nerves ever since I got here."

That halted her in her tracks. "I have? I didn't mean to be. I'm worried about getting everything done and I have to watch costs."

"That's not what I'm talking about."

"Oh." She waited for him to continue, but he didn't. "What are you talking about?"

"Why buy this place? It's a long way from Boston."

She blew out a gust of air. "That's exactly why I bought it."

He stopped working to stare at her. "Have you gotten counseling?"

His question knocked all the air out of her lungs.

She had, but she'd only gone to see the counselor twice. Both times she'd ended up having a flashback followed by a panic attack.

"It didn't help," she finally said. "It only made things worse." Her face was wet. She wiped her hand across her cheeks. When had she started crying?

"Yeah," he said softly. "It can do that the first few times."

How did he know that? The expression on his face was one she'd never seen on him before. His eyes were dark and sunken, as if old with knowledge he didn't want. Knowledge that kept wounds festering long after they should have healed.

"What happened to you?"

He put down the brush and gestured toward the doorway. "Let's take a break. Go sit in the sun."

That was the best idea she'd heard in a long time.

They settled on the terrace above the pool. Josie got them both a beer, cold from the fridge.

Neither said anything for a long couple of minutes.

Mark sighed and stared out at the distant harbor. "So my ten-year anniversary at the firehouse was about four months ago."

"Congratulations."

He shrugged with a resignation he hadn't had five years ago. Back then, he was so excited and proud to be a firefighter. "Do you remember Drake? He and I joined at the same time."

"Yeah, you and he were thick as thieves when we...dated."

"Yeah," he said with a grin that came and went. "We got into some trouble, him and I." He turned to glance at Josie. "Did you know he got married? A couple of years ago, I stood with him. Her name is Sandra and she's a teacher. Anyway, we had a three-alarm about four months ago and Drake and I were on search and rescue. It was a run-down apartment building and we weren't sure if there were any people left inside."

He took a swig of beer and she noticed his hand shaking, though his voice was strong and even. "I found an elderly woman on the floor in the first-floor hallway. I was able to get her out and get her on oxygen. She revived quick. The paramedics took over and I turned around to see how Drake had made out. He wasn't there."

Mark's voice broke, but he kept talking. "I talked to the chief, who said Drake was late by seven minutes. I asked if I could go in and get him. He told me a team of two had already been sent in."

Josie watched as Mark clenched his beer can, denting the aluminum. She leaned forward and almost put her hand on his shoulder, but caught herself before she could do it. He was in the middle of something awful and any touch, any noise from her might very well trigger a startle reaction or panic attack.

Bitter experience had taught her that the strength of the reaction had nothing to do with the person trying to help and everything to do with something no one could predict.

How a person processed horror.

Everyone experienced trauma differently, dealt with it differently, and relived it differently. There was no scale or measurement that could be applied, or pill that could dull the pain for long. For anyone who suffered from post-traumatic stress disorder, the memories were often worse in some ways than the original trauma.

Stress responses in the moment of the event are automatic, usually fast and easy to regret. Much too easy. A person might have only seconds to react during the incident, but years to lament their actions, nonactions, words said, and decisions made.

Mark was reliving the nightmare inside his head, and the bad part hadn't happened yet.

"So I waited," he said, his voice rough. "And waited. The team came out, but..." His voice trailed off.

"No Drake," she finished for him.

"No, they had him. He was..." Mark's shoulders shook. "His oxygen tank was dented. The team had found him under some debris and had dragged him out. But he lost his gloves at some point and his hands were—"

"Burned," she whispered.

Mark's voice sounded shredded. "Destroyed. No hope for recovery." He stood and threw his beer can as hard as he could.

It splashed in the pool below, but she didn't give it a second thought. She was too busy staring at Mark as he lurched back, his shoulders and legs shaking. He spun and stumbled, and ended up on his knees in front of her.

She was ready for him, her arms open.

He didn't hesitate—put his head in her lap and wrapped himself around her.

He cried for longer than she expected, but eventually, he settled down, though he kept his head where it was and his arms around her.

"I hate it when people tell me it'll get easier as time goes by," she said to him in a soft voice that allowed no argument. "Or that I did everything I could and I shouldn't feel guilty. Or that I should feel lucky, grateful because it wasn't me." She stroked his hair. "Those people, I want to punch them in the mouth."

That startled a snorting laugh out of him.

"The ones I want to choke are the ones who think that a few months is plenty of time to make everything okay," she went on, "and that I'm being dramatic or high maintenance because I have a panic attack. They don't realize that the passing of time can make it worse instead of better."

"What triggers you the most?" He sounded like he'd been eating gravel.

"Sound, most definitely. You?"

"Smell. I'm a firefighter who can't stand to smell something burning."

"Inconvenient," she said as if it were a minor inconvenience, easily dealt with.

His body started shaking again and she winced, thinking she'd triggered him again. Then he raised his head and she realized he was laughing.

Like a lunatic.

"You're the queen of understatement," he said, sitting back on the floor with his arms and legs out in front of him.

"Ha, you haven't heard nothin'. The first time I tried to go back to work a little kid slammed a bathroom door and scared the shit out of me so bad I, uh, shit my pants."

That made him roll around on the floor laughing. "The first time I tried to barbecue steaks after the fire, I threw up on the grill."

That made perfect sense to her. Still... "The poor grill."

He was laughing so hard now that tears were streaming down his face. "Not as bad as that time in college when Herbie Stubacker—the stinkiest guy I have ever met in my life—ate some kind of bean salad, and his farts after were chemical-weapon grade. It was so bad, when he let a really long one go, my buddy and I puked out the window." Mark was holding his stomach like it hurt, but that wasn't slowing down the laughter. "We were on the third floor."

"You didn't."

He nodded, laughing so hard he had to be having trouble breathing. "We did."

"Was anyone standing below you?"

He shrugged and she rolled her eyes at him. "That is the most ridiculous story you've ever told. And I'm never, *ever* serving you bean salad."

His laughter calmed a bit and he gazed at her like she was his favorite flavor of ice cream. "Thanks. You have no idea how much I needed that."

"For what? Letting you tell me stories or laughing until your sides hurt?"

He grinned. "Yes."

"I think I needed to hear what you said, too. I've been alone since Adler died. Totally alone." She sucked in a deep breath and pointed an index finger at him. "But your sister is in trouble."

"Oh yeah?"

"Yeah. She set us up."

Mark's smile turned wicked in a heartbeat. "You think?"

She pressed her lips together. "You went along with it. Why?"

"I had to get out of Boston before I self-destructed. She came to see me last week and I must have looked terrible, because she got on my ass about not taking care of myself. I told her I didn't want to hear it. Then she mentioned you, this place, and the trouble you were having with it. She thinks you can get away with saying things to me that she can't." He got to his feet. "And she's right."

Her mouth dropped open. "So, what, I'm supposed to fix you or something?"

"Nope. You work on you and I'll work on me." He started walking away. "Speaking of work, I'd better get back to it." He disappeared into the house.

She stared blankly at the ocean and did a quick self-assessment.

New life on an island in the Caribbean. *Check.*

New house and B&B. *Check.*

Hot ex-boyfriend is now man-Friday. *Check.*

Sanity. Checked out.

She dreamed of Adler dying and woke shaking in a cold sweat. A hot shower helped a little, but she felt sweaty before her coffee was ready. There was bacon and eggs in the fridge, but her stomach protested at the thought of food. Maybe some yard work would help calm her.

She stepped outside, glanced at the harbor, and realized why she was sweating already. There were deep, dark storm clouds rolling in, as if boiling up from the bottom of the ocean. The breeze was already stiff, but the question was how much worse was it going to get? There hadn't been anything worse than rain showers since she got here.

Should she board up the windows and cover the solar panels on the roof? Stock up on water and perishables? Send up a flare?

"Mark," she called out as she went back inside.

"Yeah?" His voice sounded sleep-rough from his room upstairs.

"Looks like a storm coming in," she told him. "I'm going to ask some of the locals how bad they think it might get, see if we have to batten down the hatches."

"Okay." She heard a thump on the floor above her. He'd gotten out of bed. "Coffee's hot," she said as she left, trotting down the stairs toward the shops at the bottom of the hill.

She didn't even have to ask anyone what they thought of the storm. Everyone was already closing and latching their storm shutters over windows and doors.

She stopped anyway to ask a few questions of Pirate Perry, a retired navy man who ran a gift shop/coffee bar. "Perry, how bad is it going to get? Should I worry about my solar panels? Buy extra water?"

"It's off season for a big one, but the clouds are telling a different story," he said, taking a look at them. "I'd plan for four or five days of water and food. Probably without power." He frowned at her. "Is your generator working yet?"

"Mark was sure he found the problem. Something about no maintenance and spark plugs."

"Come see me if yours isn't working. I have a backup to the backup generator I could loan you. Tell that army man of yours to knock on the back door."

Josie started back to her place. "He's a fireman, Perry, not military," she called out over her shoulder.

"I like him better already," Perry yelled back.

When she got back to The Pirate's Cay, Mark was nowhere in sight and didn't respond when she called his name, so she grabbed her purse and drove over to the grocery store. Lots of people were there stocking up on the same essentials she wanted: drinking water, canned food, bread, matches, candles, and beer. Thankfully, no one was being greedy—people weren't taking more than they could use. Obviously these people had weathered storms like this before. She threw beer in her cart because they had to have something to look forward to. Then added a bottle of whiskey for good measure.

When she got home, Mark was just walking up to the back door with a gas can in one hand and a case of bottled water in the other.

"You got the generator going?" she asked.

"Yes, ma'am. I filled it with gas, which pretty much emptied the can, so I figured I'd better fill it. Grabbed some extra water, too."

"I've got water and some other essentials in the trunk." She angled her thumb at it.

"Good job, Jo. I'll be back to help unload in a sec."

Josie started with the food, leaving it in the kitchen. By the time she got back to the car, Mark was there and had the rest in hand.

"I'm going to start closing shutters," she told him.

"I'm right behind you." His conspiratorial grin gave her an extra boost of energy.

She headed toward the front of the house, which was taking the brunt of the wind, excitement making her feel like she could run a marathon every day for the next week. She and Mark were working like a well-oiled team, anticipating what the other needed, jumping in to help without having to ask.

Just like when she and Adler...

Grief and guilt gutted her, and she came to a stumbling stop.

How could she be comparing her relationship with Mark to the one she'd had with Adler? Mark didn't love her. Still didn't, not in the way she wanted.

Guilt stabbed her again.

She couldn't breathe and didn't want to. Didn't want to ever forget why she was here in the first place.

The wind rattled the windows.

She made herself move, continue the job she'd given herself. The first shutter weighed far more than it should have. The second wasn't quite as difficult and the third seemed almost easy. By that time Mark had joined her and they worked to finish closing all the shutters around the house.

He kept looking at her out of the corner of his eye, as if he knew something was wrong, but he didn't say anything, just kept working.

The wind was really picking up, throwing plant debris and garbage around.

"Why don't you go inside?" he said in a careful tone that told her he noticed her attitude had changed. "There's only two left."

"Okay." She didn't look at him, just walked into the house.

The kitchen was a disaster. She began putting the food and water away with all the enthusiasm of a zombie chowing down at a salad bar.

The moment Mark walked in the room the temperature went up until she felt like she was swimming through pea soup.

He grabbed half of the water and took it down to the cellar. Before he left to close the last of the shutters he asked, "This is going to sound like a dumb question, but do you have a first-aid kit?"

She had to think about it. "I brought my mission kit, so yeah."

"Mission kit?"

"It's...comprehensive. I'll show you when you get back."

She heard him leave the room and sagged in relief. There was another storm blowing in, but this one wasn't outside.

Mark's heavier footsteps warned her he'd returned.

"It's a ghost town out there."

"Is it raining yet?" she asked, happy to have something as innocuous as the weather to talk about.

"Nope, but it's only a matter of time."

She filled her kettle with water and turned it on. "Tea?"

"No, thanks." He stood staring at her with one eyebrow raised, asking a question without asking a question.

"I'll show you my mission kit." She headed upstairs to one of the guest rooms then waved her hand at the pile of stuff in the middle of the room. "So, this is it."

He took in the collection of cases and bags on the floor. "Holy shit."

She winced. "Too much?"

"You could open your own ER with all this stuff."

That made her laugh, but it was a poor effort.

"What's what?" he asked.

"The big one with the wheels is a go-anywhere mass-casualty trauma station. The two backpacks are smaller, more portable versions of the trauma station. They even have flexible stretchers. The hard cases contain surgical supplies, bags of saline for IVs, a handheld blood analyzer, extra splints, bandages, and blah, blah, blah."

His gaze was steady on her face. "Blah, blah, blah, huh?"

"I know I brought too much, but where most women pack clothes and beauty products, I pack suture sets and splints."

"You're blaming this overkill of medical supplies on habit?"

"Hey." She punched him on the shoulder. "I was going to donate some of it to the local hospital or one of the clinics, but I haven't gotten around to it yet."

"Yeah, right." He danced out of range of her second punch while making a big show of rubbing his shoulder.

Ha. Like she hurt him at all. He was solid muscle. "I suppose you'd be happier if it were beer?"

"I'm a guy, that goes without saying." He was trying to be funny.

She'd lost all her funny a few minutes ago. "Time for tea," she said, leaving the room.

With the windows shuttered, the house seemed dark and smaller. She flipped on the overhead light in the kitchen and made tea. When she turned around, Mark was seated at the kitchen table with an open beer in front of him.

"Got any idea how long the storm is going to last?" he asked.

"Not a clue." She joined him at the table, shivering in the cool, damp air.

The silence was broken by the howl of the wind and lash of the rain echoing through the house. The air pressed down on her diaphragm like a too-heavy blanket and she had to force herself not to panic, to take in deep, even breaths.

"Can you imagine what it would have been like to be at sea in a storm like this?" Mark leaned forward as he asked the question, his face alight with curiosity.

"I get motion sickness," she said, focusing on his voice. "So I'm sure I know what I'd be doing."

Mark's expression turned thoughtful. "Those old sailing ships didn't have GPS or motors or radios."

"They also didn't have modern medicine, microwaves, or hot tubs."

"No hot tubs?" he asked with mock disdain. "That's it, no pirate's life for me."

She grinned. "Pansy."

"I'm a modern, fully evolved man, and I'm proud of it," he said with a nod.

"No man is fully evolved. As a gender you have a *lot* of evolving to do yet."

"Hey, I haven't once complained about breaking a nail."

She rolled her eyes.

He smiled at her, took a swig of beer then said, "It's good to have you back, Jo."

"Back? Where did I go?"

"I don't know. Back *there*. For me it was that damn apartment fire. I don't know where your personal hell is located."

A damp, cold frost settled over her, crawling down her body until it covered her entirely. Her stomach rolled and for a moment she thought she might throw up, but she took a sip of tea instead, and the warm liquid did a lot to calm her. She drank some more, small sips, with both hands wrapped around the mug.

"Syria. That's where my hell is."

Mark's jaw clenched. "I've wondered..."

He didn't finish his question, so she finished it for him. "Adler died? Yes."

"That much I knew." Mark was silent for a minute, then two. When he finally spoke again it was to ask, "Why did you go there in the first place?"

"A lot of noncombatants were being killed and injured. We were part of a large medical team to help the civilian population. We were supposed to be in a section of the country where there was no fighting, and there wasn't for the first two weeks. But that changed."

"Dangerous place," he said in a tone that was so even she knew he was bothered by it. "How did you get out?"

"American military. I have no idea what branch. I don't remember much after... Not the color of their uniforms or any of their faces." She swallowed hard, but her throat was so tight she thought she might choke. "Anyway, they got us out and home."

"How many people in your team?"

"Twenty-five."

There was another long silence.

Mark's voice was a rumble over the storm. "Benita said you quit your job. I had a hard time believing that."

"It was surprisingly easy."

"You were so passionate about working in the ER," he said, angling his head to one side as if he didn't understand her at all. "I've seen you face down drunks, drug addicts, and the damn near dead and not flinch. You have a gift for dealing with trauma cases, knowing when there was more wrong than what immediately presented."

"I *had* a gift." It still hurt her deep inside to admit she was terrified to step foot in a hospital again. "Watching violent death happen puts everything in a different perspective." She could hear the bitterness in her voice, but couldn't stop it, couldn't hide it.

"So this is your place of healing?"

She opened her mouth to tell him healing from the wound caused by Alder's death would never happen, but shut it before she could say anything.

Was coming here, fixing up The Pirate's Cay, and running a busy B&B her form of therapy? "I don't know," she finally said. "I didn't think about it like that. I just wanted something completely different from Boston."

"Well, if you've got to pick a place to do a little soul-searching and heart-healing, the Caribbean is easy on the eyes."

She gazed at his long legs stretched out in front of him as he leaned back, his T-shirt molded to his muscled arms and shoulders. He could say that again, especially since she was looking at him.

A few minutes later, Mark finished his beer then told her he was going to play with the plumbing.

Josie decided that the perfect job to keep her mind off Mark, Adler, and anything else confusing was cleaning bathrooms and got to work.

They took a break for supper—pasta and a salad. When she finished with the bathrooms, she started on the kitchen, determined to make the place shine. By the time she tumbled into bed, she was good and tired. Too tired to do more than wish Mark a mumbled good-night.

The screaming started two hours later.

Sleep didn't come quick. The sounds of the storm, howling wind, driving rain, and the rattle of trees hitting the side of the house reminded her of Syria, of the day Adler died. But after a while, she realized the storm had a pace that didn't match the hail of bullets that killed her husband. There was a rise and fall to the noise that transformed it into a full philharmonic performance.

There hadn't been music the day Adler died. It was hot and dry, the wind a sigh, until the gunfire started. Bullets pinged like hail against glass and metal all around. People yelled and shouted, some to warn, others because they'd been struck.

Someone shoved her to the ground. The cinder blocks behind her were better than armor. She called for Adler. Screamed his name over and over.

There.

He was running toward her, gesturing for her to stay where she was. Stay safe.

Another wave of bullets rained down, sending clots of dust into the air. Adler collapsed like a marionette whose strings had been cut mid-performance, his torso twisted, arms and legs splayed awkwardly.

She surged up, tried to run to him, but someone held her down, telling her she couldn't go. She watched his blood soak into the ground beneath him until there was nothing left.

Adler was dead. Dead.

She fought harder, screaming her rage and disbelief.

Hard arms wrapped around her. A man's voice called her name. Not Adler's voice, but it was a voice she trusted.

She stopped fighting to listen.

"—up. Josie, wake up!"

"Mark?" She wasn't in Syria. She was on an island in the Caribbean. There was a storm outside—rain, not bullets. Adler wasn't lying dead on the ground. He'd been buried for a year.

"God, Josie." He breathed out a huge breath. "You scared the shit out of me." He hugged her hard.

She wrapped her arms around him and breathed in his warm, musky scent. "I'm sorry."

He didn't relax a muscle. "Nightmare?"

"Yeah." Her hands clutched him tighter. "I was back there. Reliving the whole horrible—"

"We're lucky there's a storm outside or the neighbors would be calling the police."

"I wasn't just screaming in the dream?"

He rocked her back and forth. "You were yelling at the top of your lungs."

"What did I yell?"

"The only thing that made sense was your husband's name."

"Damn. I'm sorry."

"Hey." He pulled back to meet her gaze. "Don't apologize. You've got nothing to apologize for. It was the worst day of your life. Having a nightmare about it is *normal*."

She missed the warmth of his body and realized he was shirtless and wearing only a pair of boxers. "You sound like a therapist."

"I—" he intoned with great dignity, "—am the voice of reason."

A snort escaped her before she could grab it.

"Are you laughing at me?" His tone sounded incredulous.

"I would never," she replied, not quite able to keep the grin off her face.

He grinned back. "I believe you'd roll around on the floor laughing if you had only a sliver of a chance."

She shrugged.

The window rattling startled her and she pressed against him, her heart rate accelerating along with her fear.

"Whoa, I've got you," he said, smoothing one hand down her back.

"I'm so tired of being afraid," she whispered.

"Me, too. If I have to keep carrying barf bags with me when I go out on a call, I'm going to get some funny looks from the rest of the guys."

She tried to hide her smile, but wasn't too successful. Snuggling a bit closer, she put her head on his chest. His heartbeat thrummed, its tempo rising.

Then she realized that not only was he mostly naked, he was also very happy to see her. He would want to leave. She could tell by his tense muscles and hands that tried to slide her off him. She was hanging on to the here and now by the very tips of her fingers.

"Hey," Mark whispered into her hair. "I'd better get back to my own bed."

She had to convince him to stay. She took a deep breath and said, "Is there something wrong with mine?"

He cleared his throat. "No, but...shit." He squeezed her then pulled away.

She didn't even try to cooperate.

"Josie—" He tried to remove her arms from around him.

She gripped him tighter. "What?"

"I need to leave." He sounded like he was choking on the words.

The thought of being alone sent a shiver through her. "Why?"

"Because if I don't I'm probably going to do something I can't take back."

She buried her face in his neck. "I need...I need someone to hold me. Please, at least for a little while."

"Damn it." He groaned. "You're killing me, you know that, don't you?"

"Yes. No. Maybe this is payback for showing up at the airport instead of Benita."

"Hey, I had nothing to do with that stunt. I thought you knew I was coming." Mark lay down next to her and pulled her across his chest. "Come here."

Thank God. He was staying.

She snuggled close.

He petted her, running his hand over her hair. His voice was a deep rumble beneath her ear when he said, "I want to kiss you."

Every muscle in her body went on alert. No. Oh no. Bad idea. Very bad. "Why?"

"It's stupid."

Curiosity had her head off his chest and her gaze searching his face.

He was ready for her. Palming the back of her head with one hand and tilting her chin up with the other.

His lips were on hers, and he was kissing her like a marauding pirate, giving no quarter, no respite, and no escape.

She didn't want to escape.

Fright transformed into a heat that fired up the pit of her belly and spread out to warm the rest of her body. For the first time in a year, she wanted someone. Wanted Mark.

She pulled away, and he let her. They stared at each other, panting.

"Did you..." She stuttered to a stop then tried again. "Did you find the *stupidity* you were searching for?"

"Oh yeah. I discovered I'm really, *really* stupid."

A surprised laugh bubbled out of her. She slapped a hand over her mouth. "That's not funny. It isn't. Not at all."

He groaned. "I'm a complete moron."

He was not making it easy to keep a straight face. "Why do you say that?"

"Because I want you. Bad, in case you hadn't noticed."

"I may have noticed, um, some evidence of that..." She glanced at his groin and the tent his erection was making under the blankets.

"Exactly. So what do I do? I kiss you to find out if it's as good as I remember." He stopped talking.

"And?"

"It's better."

"Oh." What was she supposed to say to that? She hadn't started things. Oh, wait, yes she had. She'd screamed and then begged him to stay with her. "Do you want to go?"

He snorted and adjusted himself. "No." Then he gathered her up so her head was over his heart. "Go to sleep."

She listened to his heart beating. Its lullaby was the most beautiful thing she'd heard in a very long time.

***

Josie woke slowly and found herself tucked into Mark's arms with him spooned behind her.

She let herself just be for a while. When was the last time she had done that? Years? Mark's scent filled her nose, his taste was on her tongue and his heat wrapped around her. She could have stayed there for hours.

"You awake?" His voice was a rumble she felt all over her body.

"Maybe."

He kissed the back of her neck. "I bet I could wake you up."

"I know you could, but I'm comfortable right now."

Her stomach growled. Then so did his.

They looked at each other and started laughing.

"I need to use the washroom," she said, propping herself up on her elbows. "Maybe a shower."

"I'll start breakfast." Mark bounded out of bed. He was about to leave the room when he stopped and turned to face her. "Are we...okay?"

She'd slept, really slept for the first time in forever. She smiled at him. "Yeah, we're good."

He winked and went down the stairs.

She turned the bathroom light on, but nothing happened. She moved to the doorway to shout at Mark, but he beat her to it.

"Power's out," he hollered. "I'm going to start the generator. You might want to wait on that shower."

"Okay, thanks."

The lights came on a minute or two later and she gave herself a sponge bath with a soapy washcloth.

Josie chose a pair of khaki shorts and a short-sleeve top to wear. If the power was out, there could be damage to parts of the island or the surrounding islands, and the people on them. She might not have admitting privileges at the hospital, but she'd worked a few shifts here and there to cover for an absent doctor, seeing nothing worse than a broken bone or two.

Could be worse after this storm.

***

The storm blew out by late afternoon, but it had left its mark on the island.

Debris littered the veranda and pool. The power was still out and Mark reported a few people visible on the roads or walking around when he checked the roof. He'd gotten up there as soon as the rain started to taper off, and was very happy with himself when he discovered no damage.

Other people weren't as lucky.

As soon as the rain ended someone pounded on her door. It was a neighbor who'd cut his hand while trying to repair his own roof.

Josie took a quick look at it. "This is going to need stitches, Larry. Come in."

"I went to the hospital first, but the lineup of people waiting to be seen is down the street."

"It's okay," she said as she led him to the kitchen table, then hollered in the general direction of the veranda, "Mark, we've got customers."

He came trotting in a few seconds later. "Customers?" As soon as he saw Larry, he came to a stop. "How much of that gear do you want down here?"

"Bring the mobile trauma unit and a couple of the backpacks."

"Gotcha."

He was back with it all in a minute or two.

Josie opened the trauma unit and pulled out a suture kit and some lidocaine. "This won't take long, Larry, but you're going to have to stay off your roof for a while." She turned to Mark. "Can you let the hospital know I'm on my way over in about fifteen minutes?"

He nodded and grabbed a cell phone, but glanced at her and shook his head a few moments later. "No reception. The storm must have damaged a cell tower or something."

"Damn it."

"It'll be faster if I go over and tell them," Mark said. "If you're willing to do this kind of stuff..." He nodded at Larry's hand. "...they might be fine with you staying and working out of The Pirate's Cay."

Did she want to work in a busy ER or her own kitchen? "Yeah, I think I'd rather stay here. Having a satellite location might be useful."

Mark gave her a quick grin, and a kiss on the lips, then he was off.

Larry smirked. "I bet it would take him *two* weeks. I owe my brother some money."

Josie narrowed her eyes. "Larry, I'm a woman with a sharp needle in her hand. Now is not a good time to piss me off."

He wiped the smile off his face, but the humor was still in his voice as he said, "Yes, ma'am."

She finished with Larry and sent him on his way, then got things ready for her next patients. Either Larry or the hospital was going to send a few her way.

Four arrived at almost the same time.

One with Mark, an older lady Josie didn't know, who'd likely broken her arm.

"No power for the X-ray machine?" Josie asked when Mark explained that the triage nurse wasn't certain the woman had broken her arm.

"Yeah," he replied with a shrug.

Josie examined the woman's forearm. A pronounced bump rose from a spot about two inches up from her wrist. "Looks like a simple break to me. Let's get it splinted for now. You can have an X-ray to determine how bad or good it is when the power is back on." She glanced at Mark. "Can you triage people as they arrive?"

"Absolutely. I'm also a certified paramedic, so I'm at your disposal for whatever you need." He headed toward the front door where the three other walk-ins were waiting.

Silence from Josie's patient reigned for two whole seconds, then she said, "I'll take him if you don't want him."

"He's my fireman," Josie told her, letting her declaration settle over her. It felt right. "Get your own."

Three lacerations, two broken arms, and a concussion later, Mark brought her a cup of hot coffee and a sandwich instead of another patient.

"Eat now while you have a chance."

"Anyone waiting to see me now?"

"Yes, but you won't do anyone any good if you pass out because your blood sugar bottomed out."

She rolled her eyes. "Yes, mother." She ate her sandwich quickly and gulped down the coffee.

A half dozen people were seated outside on the veranda, waiting to be seen. She asked names and problems and put them in order of need and was about to stitch up another deep laceration in a tourist's leg when the yelling started.

"Girlie! Doctor Girlie, are you here?" A handsome man who looked like he should have been recruiting for the navy tromped onto the veranda.

"I'm right here, Captain Jack," Josie said. "What do you need?"

"A doctor."

"For what?"

"We need some first-aid supplies and a pair of hands who know how to use them on the island."

"What kind of injuries?"

"A couple of people got cut up pretty bad and one guy broke his hand."

"I can go," Mark offered.

Did she want him to? People were injured. Could she say no?

Her stomach wound around itself until it hurt and her breathing became so painful it was all she could do to take one more breath.

"You can't have him for long," she told Jack. "Grab one of the backpacks and come back as soon as you can," she said to Mark.

He nodded. "Can I have a minute before I take off?"

She followed him into the house and up the stairs to one of the bedrooms. "Is something wrong?"

He turned to face her. "I'm coming back."

"You darn well better. I need you here."

He sighed. "That's not what I mean."

"I don't—"

He took her by the shoulders, interrupting her. "I'm coming back, not shot. Not hurt. Do you understand?"

"I never thought—"

"I can see it in your eyes." Mark's voice was a low rumble. "The worry, the fear. You've been having flashbacks since Larry showed up." Mark bent until he was nose to nose with her. "I'm fine and I'm going to stay that way."

She should have known he, of all people, would understand. "I can't stop it." She rubbed her forehead. "I can't shut it off, and I don't know how long I can keep it together before I break."

"I know something that will help, at least for a little while."

"What's that?"

"This." He kissed her, gently for the first two seconds, then he groaned, yanked her up against him, and plundered her mouth. Desire and need burned through the chill haze of memory that had her in its grasp, wiping it from her mind. All she knew was Mark's taste, scent, and the firmness of his muscles under her hands.

He pulled away to stare into her eyes. "When I get back, we're going to finish this *conversation*." He leaned down to whisper in her ear, "It might take a couple of days."

A shiver went through her. "You don't pull your punches, do you?"

"No." His gaze was as steady as the Rock of Gibraltar. "I know what I want."

She took in a deep, shaky breath. He hadn't known before, when he left her all those years ago. "Okay."

One of his eyebrows rose.

"Okay," she said, putting some steel into her voice.

"Don't forget," he said when she would have turned to leave.

She snorted. "I won't. That kiss damn near caused me to have a seizure. You should come with a warning label."

His grin was all kinds of bad. "Where would be the fun in that?"

Shaking her head, she led the way downstairs and watched as Mark grabbed one of the backpacks and followed Captain Jack out of the house.

Josie went back to work, but kept watching for his return.

He wasn't gone five minutes and she missed him already.

A steady stream of people needing medical care flowed through the house, most of them locals, but a few were tourists who were staying at other B&Bs close by. Every single one of them asked why she was opening a B&B when she was an experienced trauma doctor.

She told them she'd gotten tired of seeing death.

Most of the locals also asked about Mark. The women wanted his cell phone number or wanted to leave their cell phone numbers. The men wanted to know if he was a full-time roofer and was he interested in a little work on the side.

She told them not until The Pirate's Cay was finished.

She closed the door on the last patient at about 10:00 p.m.

Cleaning up took a little while, maybe an hour, then the only thing she was left with for company was the wind and the sigh of palm trees.

The stack of first-aid cases she'd shoved to one side of the kitchen drew her attention despite her efforts to not look at them at all.

The memory of Adler laughing at something she'd said while packing those cases over a year ago taunted her. She caught her breath, bracing herself for the rest of the flashback, but the feel of Mark's lips on hers pushed it out of focus.

Trembling, she turned away, climbed the stairs, and went into her bathroom. Sweat had dried on her skin, but it felt like desert sand. Washing it off was the only way she had to break the cycle of memories trying to pull her under.

Mark's kiss was another, but he wasn't here. Not yet.

Water, steam, and soap washed her clean, but her stubborn mind wouldn't let go of the memory spiral.

Mark's voice calling her name gave her a lifeline. It took her a moment to realize it wasn't a figment of her imagination, but real, in the here and now.

She shut off the water and called out, "I'm in the shower."

Footfalls on the stairs had her stumbling out of the shower and drying herself off as fast as she could.

He was in her room now, his footsteps approaching the bathroom door. She wrapped a towel around her body. The door opened and she launched herself at him.

"Josie, are you— Oomph." He rocked back on his feet as she glommed on to him, burying her nose against his shirt to breathe in his scent and the scent of the sea.

His arms came around her, enveloping her in their warm strength. "Are you okay?"

"Yes. No." She leaned back and tried to pull his head down. "I need your kiss."

His lips were on hers and she dropped every shield, every barrier and took him inside where he could fight the desert demons of her own thoughts.

His groan mirrored her own as he kissed her like she was more necessary than breathing. One of his hands landed on her ass where the towel had rode up. Those fingers clenched on her, tugging her against him.

He pulled his head back. "Josie," he said, breathing heavily. "Slow down."

"Don't want to go slow."

"Babe, we need to talk for a minute."

She was breathing so hard she could barely talk. "Why?"

"Because you're dressed in almost nothing, you look like a wet dream, I'm hard as a rock, and we're about to do something neither of us can take back."

"I need you, your kiss. You promised."

"I did and I'm yours," he growled. "But I want all of you in return."

She looked up at him. The veneer of safe male was gone, leaving a pirate in his place with wild eyes and a wicked grin, and she made her decision. "Are you afraid of me?"

He swallowed hard. "You're the most dangerous woman I know."

"You're the most dangerous man I know, but I want you to stay."

His eyebrows went up. "Yeah?"

"Yeah." She stroked one index finger from his neck down his chest. "I'm tired of being afraid of myself, tired of feeling alone, tired of feeling sad."

"You're playing with fire." His voice rumbled out of his chest. "Be sure, Josie. I don't want you to regret this in the morning or any day after."

"I'm touch starved and you're the only man alive I trust enough to…" She caught her breath. Had she said too much? Would he run away if he realized how badly she needed him? He'd run before.

"To what?" he prompted as he took her hand and guided it down to the waistband of his jeans.

She undid the button and slid down the zipper. He wasn't running. At least not yet. "To burn away my tattered edges, to release the real me from the prison I put myself in. I've felt nothing but grief for the past year. I'll kill myself if I keep going on like this." She slung one hand around his neck and stretched up until she was almost kissing him. She hooked fingers into his underwear, pulled the top back, and slid her hand inside to stroke his cock. "Free me," she whispered against his lips.

Would he run now or take what she was offering?

He groaned and exploded into action, jerking her close and kissing her like she was his only source of oxygen.

Sensation washed over her, chasing the chill of despair away, heating her blood until she thought she might set them both on fire.

His hands held her close with a strength that should have frightened her, but made her feel safe instead. One of those big hands moved from her back to her torso to cup a breast and she moaned as he flicked his thumb over her nipple.

Hungry lips moved from her mouth, down her neck, to her collarbone and into the valley between her breasts. He pulled back long enough to snatch at the towel she was wearing and throw it aside.

He caught her, his hands spanning her rib cage just below her breasts. He stared at them for a long moment, then his gaze moved up to meet her own. "I love your breasts."

Breathing was optional, wasn't it? "I remember."

He laid her out on the bed very carefully. Then he looked her over, from her toes to the tips of her hair. "Fucking gorgeous." He ran his hands over her as if he were a blind man relearning her body all over again.

"Mark?"

"Darlin'?"

"You're going too slow."

He grinned and started taking his clothes off. "Really? Are you sure? 'Cause slow can be a lot of fun."

His shirt hit the floor. His muscles were more defined than she remembered. She licked her lips. "I've decided fast has its place."

"What place would that be?" His jeans and underwear were next.

His cock, as large as the rest of him, drew her hands like a magnet. "The one where I get to enjoy multiple orgasms."

Laughing, he joined her on the bed, grabbed her wrists, and planted them on either side of her head while he kissed and nipped at her bottom lip, her chin, neck, and breast. When he got to her nipple he paused to play, sucking, nipping, and sucking again, until she arched under him. Every touch drove her higher, wound her tighter, until all she could do was shake.

"I want to touch you," she managed to say, her voice quivering as he caught both wrists in one grip and sent his other hand down to stroke into her heated core.

"You can touch me...later. After the first three or four... God, you're slick. And hot." His breathing became erratic.

He leaned away to grab something out of his pants. A condom. He put it on then came back to her, his hands tormenting her again.

She twisted against him, trying to find what she needed, but what she needed was more. "Mark, stop teasing me. I need..." She paused, the words drying up in her throat as he pressed his cock at the entrance to her body and pushed inside. "That," she moaned. "That's what I need."

He paused after he'd seated himself inside her. "Fuck."

"Yes, please," she replied and deliberately tightened the muscles surrounding him.

"God damn, I like it when you talk dirty," he told her as he pulled out and stroked in, setting a relentless pace that had her orgasm hovering for what felt like forever.

"Please," she begged. "Faster."

He groaned. "You're killing me, Josie."

"I'm going to if you don't—" The words died in her throat as he stepped up the pace, giving her what she needed, and her orgasm rolled over her.

Gasping, tears rolling down her face and shaking, she held on to him. When his own orgasm overtook him, holding him rigid above her, his head thrown back, she found herself fascinated and hungry for him all over again.

He sank down to kiss her languidly, like he had all the time in the world.

She kissed him back, not knowing how long the calm inside her was going to last.

***

Morning arrived with pounding on the front door.

Josie cracked one eye open and glanced at her watch. 6:00 a.m. Nope, she wasn't getting up. If it was an emergency, the police could blare their siren. Then she'd get up.

The pounding continued.

Mark swore as he rolled out of bed and landed on the floor with a thump. Josie heard some scuffles, more swearing, then he stood up wearing only his jeans and stomped down the stairs.

A few seconds later she heard him yell, "What?"

Masculine voices rumbled, but not loud enough for her to make out individual words, but if Mark was actually talking to whoever was at the door, that someone was probably going to insist on her getting out of bed.

She went to the bathroom and brushed her teeth. When she came out, Mark was waiting for her.

"Who was that?" she asked.

"Someone from the hospital," he said in a cautious tone. "They're asking if you'll work in the ER today."

"They run out of doctors?"

"No. They have too many patients."

The worst medical case she'd seen on the two shifts she'd worked at the St. Thomas hospital was sunstroke in a two-year-old. Today would be more of yesterday, times ten.

"I barely held myself together yesterday. The only thing that kept me from falling apart was your..." She caught herself. Dare she finish the sentence? Confess how much she needed him?

"My...what?"

She stared into his eyes, watching for a reaction to her next word. "Kiss." She shrugged. "You were right. The tactile memory kept me from imploding."

"That was here, in your home," he said, meeting her gaze. "Where you feel relatively safe."

He was right again. She did feel safe here, and yet the PTSD almost knocked her to her knees yesterday.

"I can't do it. There are too many triggers at the hospital."

"That's what I told the guy waiting downstairs," Mark said with a short nod. "So I asked about the older people on the island. The ones who need a medical check, but aren't mobile enough to get to the hospital without assistance. He said they can't spare anyone to check on the homebound." Mark let that sink in for a second then asked, "What do you think, Jo, want to offer to do some house calls? I can be your man-Friday."

"You're already my man-Friday, and I think it's a brilliant idea. Let's do it."

Clothes. She needed clothes, something that said both professional and island. She settled on a pair of khaki pants with way too many pockets and another short-sleeved collared shirt, also with pockets.

"We've got to get the hospital on board with the idea first."

"Somehow I don't think it's going to take a lot of convincing to allow a doctor to take care of patients in their homes instead of those people overtaxing emergency responders who are already too busy. We've got all the medical supplies we should need downstairs. A quick restock and we can be ready to go." She pulled on socks and found her hiking shoes in the closet. Right about then, she realized Mark was still in his jeans and nothing else. "What?"

There was a small smile on his face. "I love you."

The shoes tumbled out of her hands.

Mark strode close and knelt in front of her. He took her hands in his and that's when she realized her hands were shaking. "It's okay," he said softly. "No pressure, I promise. I just want you to know where I stand."

"But you..." she began. "You've only been here a week, you can't possibly..."

"I never stopped."

"Stopped?"

"Loving you. I never stopped." He shook his head. "I was an idiot for telling you I wasn't ready to settle down five years ago. By the time I realized I loved you, really-deeply-for-the-rest-of-my-life loved you, it was too late. You'd met Adler and he'd given you the commitment you needed."

Her mouth was open, but she couldn't speak.

"I won't leave here without being completely convinced you don't love me back," he told her. "Captain Jack gave me a few pointers on how to be a good pirate yesterday." He leaned forward until his forehead rested against hers and whispered, "I plan on stealing your heart."

She freed one hand so she could cup his face and run her thumb over his bottom lip. "You already did, you damn pirate. I love you."

He kissed her, heaved a huge sigh then got to his feet and pulled her to hers. "All right then, girlie, time to get to work. This ain't no vacation."

"Excuse me, mate," Josie told him with her hands on her hips. "But I be captain of this ship. I'm the one giving orders."

"Right you are, sir," Mark said, slipping his arms around her. "And what would your orders be?"

"Kiss me *then* we'll get to work."

"Aye, sir. Vacation first it is then."

"It's a kiss," she said, laughing. "A minute or two is *not* a vacation."

He leaned down to whisper against her lips, "It is if you do it right."

Epilogue

One year later...

Josie parked the car behind the house and began hauling in the groceries. "Mark, can you give me a hand?" she called as she shouldered her way in through the backdoor.

No answer.

"Mark?"

The house gave no response.

He must be busy with something out of ear shot. His sister, Benita, who just happened to be her best friend, had stayed with them for a couple of weeks and been a huge help, but she'd gone home a month ago. She planned to return to give them a hand again in few weeks. It was the least she could do for instigating the situation Josie found herself in right now.

Exhaustion dogged her constantly, even when her fingers itched to reorganize the linen closet or kitchen pantry.

It took her a few trips to bring in all the bags of fresh fruit, flour and all the makings of homemade cinnamon buns and bread they needed for the next week of guests to the inn. They were fully booked, over booked even.

She was beginning to wish for a stable, horses included, for any possible overflow.

Mark had discovered a hidden talent for bread making and now ruled the kitchen with a pastry chef's confidence. Spending so much time in the kitchen, baking delicious pastries had helped him cope with his reaction to the scent of something burning. Josie had taken a workshop on creating flowers and other sculpted art out of fruit, and found a whole new use for her exceptional manual dexterity. Instead of sewing wounds or surgery, she now dazzled people with her vegetable landscapes and watermelon effigies. The result had given the inn a reputation of satisfying both the eyes and the stomachs of their guests.

Speaking of which, Mark's current batch of sweet dough was ready to be kneaded again.

"Mark?" she hollered again. "Your dough is done."

"Coming." His voice sounded far away, like he was outside.

Probably watering the plants. He loved growing things.

She sat down with a thump on a chair in the kitchen to rest her aching feet and back, and catch her breath.

A few seconds later Mark came into the kitchen, but instead of rushing to the bowl of dough, he went straight to Josie. "How are you feeling? Lightheaded? Dizzy?" He put his fingers over her pulse.

She rolled her eyes. "I'm fine." One of her hands stroked her belly. She hadn't seen her feet in weeks. "Just tired. I'm more than ready for this baby to arrive."

He leaned in and kissed her. "Just a couple more weeks to go." He bent down a little and said to their baby, "Give your mom a break, will ya, squirt?"

"Stop calling the baby that," she said, rolling her eyes. "He or she is going to think their name is squirt."

"I've got to call the kid something. When are we going to decide on the names?"

"I like the boy's name you suggested. Ben."

Mark grinned. "Awesome, Benita will probably go nuts over it."

"Any suggestions for a girl's name."

A sneakier smile flirted with the corners of his lips. "Wilma?"

"No."

"How about one of those trendy names like Aisha or Sparkles?"

"Sparkles?" Josie asked him with a shake of her head, trying not to laugh. "I'm not naming my possible daughter after a horse." She sighed and put her head on the table. "Tired."

"Would you like some tea and a slice of fresh bread?" Mark's voice vibrated with his desire to care for her. It lifted her spirits despite how tired she felt.

"The doctor said no bread."

"He also said no cookies, potatoes or rice, which I think is crazy." Mark put his hands up as if in surrender. "How is a man supposed to provide whatever weird food craving the pregnant mother of his child demands?"

She struggled not to smile. "Wow, it's hard to be you." She went to stand, but a dizzy spell convinced her to stay seated. "I'd like that tea and bread. I'm famished."

"Are you sure you're okay?" Mark asked as he placed a mug and plate in front of her.

"Yes." She patted his hand. "We pregnant ladies are more and more easily tired as our due date approaches."

Her baby chose just that moment to kick a few times, hard enough that the movement was visible through her shirt.

"Whoa." Mark put his hand over the spot just in time to feel another series of kicks, and grin hugely. "Someone has plenty of energy."

"It never fails. As soon as I sit down to rest, the baby decides it's time to play hopscotch in there." She took a bite of Mark's delicious homemade bread and sipped her tea. "Mmm. Your bread is so goooood."

He leaned in and kissed her lingeringly on the neck. "Watching you eat," he whispered as he kissed her again. "Makes me hungry for something other than food."

She snorted. "Ha. I look like a house." What did he see? The question had been on her mind for a while because he was just as amorous now, if not more, than before she got pregnant.

He leaned back to meet her gaze. "You're kidding, right?"

She gave him a helpless smile and shook her head.

"You look at yourself and see...?"

She filled in his blank with, "A huge, walking blimp."

"I see sexy curves and my child." His smile was sinful. "You're a lush goddess I want to worship." He leaned forward to kiss her with a sensual slide of his lips against hers. "What does my goddess desire?" he asked, kissing and nibbling on her neck.

"I want…" she breathed, putting a hand behind his head to hold him to her. "More bread."

His body shook with laughter as he pulled back to plant another kiss on her mouth. "I live to serve you, my goddess" he managed to get out between snorts.

Another slice of bread and a cup of hot tea later and she was feeling a little more energetic. She started work on carving a huge flower out of a large watermelon, but had to sit down after only a few minutes. The muscles of her back were screaming at her, but after a few minutes, the pain let up a bit.

When the pain returned after ten minutes, she closed her eyes and took an inventory of her body.

Thirty six weeks pregnant. Check.

Baby dropped into position. That happened last week. Check.

Returning muscle pain in her back. Check.

Chances of her beginning labor. Damn good.

Shit. She wasn't ready. There were still things she wanted to do before the baby came. Another coat of paint in the nursery, the purchase of a stroller and another dozen other small jobs. She wasn't even finished with the job in front of her. She'd say something as soon as she finished this watermelon.

So she could give birth to her own melon. That thought made her giggle.

She was still laughing to herself when Mark walked back into the kitchen. "What's so funny?"

"Oh, just that I'm really working on two melons right now, rather than one," she said pointing at her belly and the fruit sculpture she was putting the finishing touches on.

He stared at her for a moment with the expression a man makes only when he suspects a woman has been drinking too much.

That made her laugh harder and she rocked back and forth in her chair.

The muscles of her back seized again, this time it spread around and across her pelvis, making her gasp.

A gush of fluid flowed down her legs to rain onto the floor.

"Jo?" Mark asked walking toward her. "Was that your–"

"Yup," she said breathing through the contraction. "It's official, I'm in labor."

When he didn't move, just stood and stared with a frozen face, she asked conversationally, "You're not going to be one of those guys who loses his marbles as soon as his partner goes into labor, are you?"

He swallowed. Hard. "I can't promise anything at this point." He tried to smile, but it sort of wobbled on his face, like he couldn't keep a hold of it.

Oh, dear. "Well, don't. Come over here and help me to the couch. I want you to see how dilated I am." She held out a hand, and when he didn't move fast enough for her liking, waved it around. "Captain's orders."

He helped her to her feet and walked with her to the couch.

She tried to grab her underwear under her dress, but that wasn't happening. "Take my panties off please."

Mark started to laugh. "That I can do."

"You're such a guy."

He snorted, but got her underwear off then ducked down to look between her legs. "Holy shit."

She waited to find out what his exclamation meant, but when no further information came from him she asked, "Is that a *good* holy shit, or a *bad* holy shit?"

"It's a *you're almost fully dilated* holy shit." Mark pulled his head back and looked at her. "We aren't going to make it to the hospital."

Holy shit was right. Another contraction gripped her right then and she was too busy trying to breathe through it to argue.

Mark held her hands for a moment, then as the contraction was easing, told her he'd be right back and dashed off.

This was not a good time to run an errand.

She was going to yell out for him, but another contraction began not even a minute after the last one ended.

Her stomach dropped. This was happening much too fast.

Mark returned with one of her treatment bags. He opened it up and began pulling stuff out of it.

Josie had to focus to keep from groaning with the strength of the contraction. It felt like her whole body was involved in it, trying to squeeze the baby out.

"I want to push," she gasped out.

Mark ducked between her legs again. "Don't. Wait, okay? Can you wait until the next contraction?"

"I'll," she huffed out as she tried to talk her body into some kind of truce. "Try."

"We need to get you off of this couch and onto the floor," Mark muttered.

"Good luck with that," she managed to croak out, still caught in the grip of the contraction.

There was a loud knock from somewhere in the vicinity of the front door.

"The couch is too bouncy," Mark said to her, ignoring the noise. He came around to stand just behind her, and as her contraction eased, she managed to assist in getting herself onto the floor.

Mark arranged her limbs, took a look between her legs and pronounced, "This is much better."

"Why isn't anyone answering the door?" an irate masculine voice demanded.

Josie didn't even look to see who it was, she recognized Captain Jack's voice. "Because I'm having the baby right *now*," she told him a little louder than she intended. Another contraction gripped her and she found it hard to breathe let alone speak.

The urge to push was even stronger this time, so when she began to bear down, Mark encouraged her.

"That's it, honey. Push!"

There was more, along with a short, but irritating argument between Mark and Jack about moving her or going for help. Finally Jack disappeared, which suited her just fine. All the noise was distracting.

Her child was almost here, and despite the pain she couldn't *wait* to hold the baby.

After what seemed like hours, she felt a sudden lessoning of the pressure and Mark yelled, "The head is out."

The contraction eased a little and she took that opportunity to gulp in as much air as possible before the next one began.

"Just the shoulders left, Jo," Mark said with a determined expression. "Almost there."

She wasn't worried. Having him here, delivering their baby, made her feel safer than if she'd been in the hospital. "Okay," she said, puffing, then nodded as the next contraction had her pushing again. This time it didn't take long, only a few seconds, before the baby slipped out of her and into Mark's waiting hands.

"We have a little girl," Mark said, the widest grin she'd ever seen on his face. "God, Jo, she's gorgeous."

He was busy with the baby, then she suddenly let out a cry. A strong, healthy cry.

A few seconds later, Mark wrapped the baby in a towel and set her into Josie's arms.

Tiny face. Eyes of a deep blue that seemed to look right into her soul and hands that wrapped around her finger at the first touch. Her baby girl.

"She has your nose," she said to him, smiling.

"And your bossiness," Mark laughed. Their daughter was still crying, but he was right, it had a distinct demanding tone to it.

"They're right through there," Captain Jack said.

A moment later, two men dressed in Emergency Services uniforms came into the room.

"You missed the big show," Josie told them. "By about five minutes."

The two men shrugged.

"As long as we've got a healthy baby, that's what counts," one of the paramedics said.

"If anyone was going to have a home birth, you two are the most qualified to deal with it," the other one said. "Boy or girl?"

"Girl," Mark answered, his voice ringing with pride.

"What are you calling her?"

Mark looked at Josie and she smiled. "I'm going to name her after the smarty pants responsible for bringing us together. Tia. Her name is Tia Durant."

Book Three
Medal of Honor

* * *

Three days before Christmas, a burned-out Chicago detective adds a new homicide to the pile of active cases on his desk—a homeless man gunned down in an alley. The case hits him hard when he discovers the victim is an Army vet and a Medal of Honor recipient. He and the victim's estranged daughter have to work fast to find the killer, because she's next on his kill list. As they investigate the murder, they discover their fathers served together in Vietnam and they share the same Native American heritage. This warrior and medicine woman will need a miracle to evade the evil stalking them, but during the season of love, anything is possible.

* * *

Medal of Honor

Dead men tell no tales, but this guy wasn't done talking yet.

Chicago detective George Eaglefeather crouched next to the homeless man struggling to breathe on the ground of a dank, dark alley. Wrinkles around his eyes and mouth caught and shadowed the weak street light fifty feet or so away, making him look washed out and skeletal. Thinning hair, long and limp, and a scraggly beard made it almost impossible to distinguish his facial features. He could have been anywhere from sixty to one hundred and ten years old.

"No, no. Ali, I'm sorry." The words were garbled and slurred. There was blood all over the guy's clothing and the ground underneath him.

"Sir," George said, grabbing the man's bloody hand. "Who did this to you?"

The grip on George's hand was strong enough to make him wince.

"Tell Allison I'm sorry." Frothy blood bubbled out of his mouth and dribbled down the side of his chin. He tried to lift his head, but it only wobbled before gravity brought it back to the alley's oily asphalt.

Goddamn it, no one deserved to die like this, as if he were another piece of garbage tossed aside with a casual cruelty he'd seen far too much of this past year. "Who's Allison?" George asked, putting his face in the man's line of sight.

Instead of answering, the homeless man shoved a paper bag at him.

George took it and glanced down at the crumpled mess. When he raised his head, the homeless man was dead, his eyes fixed on a point the living couldn't see.

Shit. Who the hell was Allison? Wife? Mother? Daughter? The waitress at his favorite diner?

He looked the body over. The victim was probably wearing three or four layers of clothing, all of it crusted in dried mud and torn like he'd been hiding in a hole in the ground. He reeked of sweat, smoke, and human filth.

Murder was a dirty business. That this one took place three days before Christmas added an extra level of grime. Christmas was a time to show your fellow man mercy and forgiveness, but there was no mercy in this crime. The victim had nothing of value. Why kill him?

The callousness of the killing started a slow burn under George's skin. Didn't people have better things to do than kill each other? You know, like donate money to a shelter or toys to kids?

Behind him, the fading wail of an ambulance echoed down the alley and the lights of the vehicle bounced off the cement walls of the surrounding buildings.

George stood and faced the paramedics running toward him. "Sorry, fellas." Did he sound as tired as he felt? As disgusted? "This one is destined for the morgue."

"Great. Why didn't you radio it in?" one of them asked.

"He just passed." With no one at his side besides a burned-out detective who had been shocked into giving a shit for the first time in months. "Poor bugger."

Grumbling, the paramedics walked their gurney back to their vehicle, passing two uniformed cops on their way in.

"Hey, Feather," one of them said. "What have we got... Whoa, what a stench." He stopped and took a couple steps back.

"He's a murder victim," George told them. Where was their respect for the dead? "I was eating at the sushi place right across the street. Two shots and I was out the door, but the perp was already gone, and the victim was still breathing."

"Mugging gone wrong?"

"I don't think so." George clenched the paper bag tighter in his hand. "Someone named Allison was important enough to make her name almost his last word."

"Have you called in the coroner and forensics guys?"

"Not yet. Do you mind doing that?"

One of the uniforms shrugged. "Sure."

George walked out of the alley, then pulled a flashlight out of his car parked across the street. He returned and began a grid search of the area around the murdered man. It would have been nice to find something useful like blood drops, shoe impressions, or even shell casings from the bullets that had ended the homeless man's life, but all he found were bits of garbage. Nothing seemed pertinent to the case.

This was not what he wanted for Christmas—one more unsolved murder to add to the stack on his desk. George grunted. Somehow he'd made it onto Santa's naughty list, no doubt thanks to his ex-wife. Last year she'd given him divorce papers on Christmas Day. It had gutted him. He'd known she was unhappy, but didn't have a clue how bad it was until he opened the shoe box with the documents inside. He'd been planning to take her on a vacation to somewhere hot with a beach. He'd thrown himself into work instead. Now it was a year later and he still didn't know what the fuck he wanted out of life.

He was just as homeless as the dead man on the ground in front of him. Sure he might have a place to sleep, but he didn't have a *home*.

The coroner and forensics guys arrived at the same time. George could have gone to his apartment for a few hours of sleep, but he couldn't get the victim's face out of his head. That sad, tired, and haggard expression made him itch to find the asshole responsible. Besides, the morgue with its sterile area and operating room lighting was a better place to examine the paper bag and its contents.

Thirty minutes later, he watched the coroner and his assistant begin to undress the corpse.

"I'll get you a time of death as soon as we get his clothes off," the coroner, Dr. Bashir, said.

"Don't bother. I was there when he died." Somehow this sterile room, with its bright lights and empty echoes, seemed just as wrong a place for the dead as the alley. "He kept trying to apologize to someone named Allison. Handed me this bag. I only took my eyes off him for a couple of seconds, but by the time I glanced back at him, he was gone."

"Huh. Well, that's a time saver," Bashir said with a pleased nod. He and his assistant rolled the dead man over and finished removing the first layer of clothing. It took them ten more minutes to get the last layer off—a ratty T-shirt with what looked like some kind of military crest on it.

"Well, I'll be damned," Bashir whispered in a revered tone George had never heard the guy use. Ever.

"What?"

"Is this real?" If anything, his tone was even more amazed.

George stepped forward and damned near genuflected at what he saw around the homeless man's neck.

A Medal of Honor.

An honest-to-God Medal of Honor.

"Can I see his T-shirt again?" George asked the coroner.

The other man handed George the article of clothing without comment.

He unfolded it and stared hard at the remaining ink. "This is a Green Beret crest," he said, staring at the homeless man's body. The slow burn that had started back in the alley ignited into something dark and dangerous. "Someone murdered a hero."

"You don't think this guy could have stolen the shirt or medal?"

George snorted. "Never happen. Besides, he was wearing it under his clothes. He wasn't showing it off, and he couldn't have bought it anywhere. No, this was his."

"How many men alive have one of those?" the coroner asked.

"One less than yesterday." George had to work to keep the snarl out of his voice. He'd save his anger for the murderer. He took the paper bag and set it on an unused exam table, opening it carefully and allowing the contents to fall out.

Several pieces of newspaper—some folded, others crumpled—lay on top. George put on a pair of gloves and began separating them.

Underneath all the paper was a pendant. He turned it over and rubbed a layer of grime off the front.

A blue tiger's eye. It looked old-fashioned, antique, but not expensive. An odd thing for a homeless man to hang on to.

He began reading the newspaper clippings. They were all about the same person—a surgeon named Allison Stoneman.

Stoneman? Where had he heard that name before? A memory teased him with clarity before it hid behind the smoke and mirrors that was the mind's refuge.

Her picture appeared with several of the articles and he found himself captured by her wide-set intelligent eyes and triangular face. A beautiful woman.

Chances were good that this surgeon was the same woman the victim had been trying to apologize to right before he died. A mission he'd given to George with the handoff of the bag.

George's soldiering days were long over, but he couldn't ignore a request from a Medal of Honor recipient any more than he could allow his murder to go unpunished.

"Two shots to the chest," the coroner said with an edge to his tone that told George he found this murder as unacceptable as he did. "Looks like nine millimeter. The shots weren't through and through. I'll get the slugs to ballistics as soon as I find them."

"Thanks, Doc. I'm going to track down this Allison Stoneman. Can you let forensics know this bag and contents are evidence? I'd like to know if there's any trace on this stuff that might explain why he was killed."

"Will do."

George left the morgue, then pulled out his battered tablet to do a search for Dr. Stoneman. According to the search engine, she worked at a VA hospital not far from the precinct. He called the hospital and was told she was on duty, but in surgery and wouldn't be out for several hours. Forensics contacted him shortly after to let him know that the dead man's fingerprints matched a man named Arthur Stoneman, no known address, Army veteran.

George's next call was to a friend who was an active-duty recruiting officer for the Army.

"Hey, Meathead, it's Feather. How are things?" Meathead was an apt nickname for a man whose hat size was larger than most men's IQs.

"About as good as it gets in uniform. What's the emergency?"

"How do you know there is one?"

"It's ten thirty at night. You don't work one second past your shift schedule unless shit's hit the fan."

"Yeah, okay, you got me there. I need some background info on a murder victim, a homeless vet. Some asshole shot him a few hours ago."

"Homeless? Got a name?"

"Arthur Stoneman. He had a Medal of Honor around his neck."

"Ah, damn." Charles "Meathead" Murphy sighed. "Art was a Vietnam vet in his early sixties. Green Beret. Received the Medal of Honor for turning himself into a human shield while getting seven other soldiers out of an ambush. Sustained three bullet wounds in the process. In and out of the VA, but he'd mostly been out on the street for the last couple of years."

"You knew him personally?"

"I kept track of him. It was a sin to see a man of his courage so...broken."

Interesting observation. "What broke him?"

The laugh that came out of Meathead sounded tired and old. "Surviving."

"Is that what got him killed?" If he was suffering from PTSD, sometimes surviving was worse than getting killed in action.

"Don't know. He was quiet, kept to himself, and was really good at disappearing into a crowd. He had almost no family, just a daughter."

"Did he have any kind of relationship with his daughter?"

"Not that I could tell, but he never went too far from the VA hospital where she works."

George had never met a man who didn't have a relationship with at least one person, good or bad. "He shadowed her?"

"Probably. Art told me once that they didn't have much contact at his request. He didn't say it out loud, but he made it clear that he didn't think he was good for her."

"Paranoid or justified?" Many homeless vets were on the street because they didn't trust the people around them. Or they didn't know which ones to trust.

"It's hard to tell with the guys who go over the edge. And Art was all the way over. All he saw were friendlies and bad guys, and as time went by, fewer and fewer people stayed friendlies. He didn't even want to talk to me the last time I saw him." Meathead sighed. "He thought I was being followed."

"Maybe the daughter can help me figure out who was who."

"Maybe." Meathead paused for a long couple of seconds. "I hope you catch the guy who killed Art. He won the medal because he risked his life and took bullets for other soldiers. When it came to helping other people, he was fearless. It was himself he couldn't, or wouldn't, save."

"You know me. I'm a three-year-old with a ball of cotton candy when I'm on a case. Once I've had a taste, I'm not letting go or giving it up." His ex-wife put it differently, said he had OCD for his work. Wouldn't eat or sleep until it was done. It wasn't a compliment.

"Good." Meathead ended the call.

Time to meet Allison.

The hospital ER was busy, but the hallway outside the OR was deserted. A passing nurse told him Allison was still in surgery, but she'd check to see how much longer the surgeon would be.

George leaned against the wall and let his mind relive the moments before Arthur Stoneman died. The sound of the shots had him out of the small restaurant and sprinting across the street. He'd slowed once inside the alley, but the gasping from the body on the ground had pulled him forward. The terror in the dying man's eyes. The strange rattle of his breathing. The moment of complete silence when he died.

No matter how many times he'd witnessed death, he would never get used to the sensation of a person going from a living thing to one that wasn't. The spirit gone. The body nothing more than a cooling carcass.

Sometimes, he hated his job.

***

Allison stripped off her bloody gloves and threw them in the garbage. The mask and OR scrubs went into the soiled linen bin. Twelve hours of surgery had left her with a sore back and burning shoulders. She needed something hot to drink—tea, not coffee—and something sweet and cinnamony to eat.

But she wasn't going to get either because there was a detective waiting for her and no one would tell her why.

That was never a good sign.

She checked on her patient in the recovery room then trudged out to talk to the cop.

He was leaning against the wall, his sleeves rolled up and his suit jacket hooked on a finger and hanging over his shoulder. He saw her and straightened, broad shoulders straining the fabric of his shirt. Dark eyes met hers and she took note of his blade of a nose and chiseled cheekbones.

They had something in common. He was descended from Native Americans, same as she was.

"I'm Allison Stoneman," she said in a professional tone and held out her hand. "You're here to see me?"

"Yes. Detective George Eaglefeather." He took her hand and shook it twice, while searching her face with a gaze that seemed to see to the bottom of her soul. "You were in surgery a long time. Are you on a break now?"

Surprise and relief flooded her system. He wasn't one of those cops who didn't care about someone else's schedule. She'd seen too many of those interviewing battered women during her residency. "I'm off work now, actually, but I need to eat."

"You look a little peaked, as my Irish grandmother used to say. I think you need some food in your belly. Is there somewhere quiet where we could talk and eat at the same time around here?" he asked as he glanced at his watch. "At twelve thirty in the morning."

He wanted to talk *and* feed her. The news must either be really bad or complicated. "There's a pancake house a three-minute walk from here," she suggested.

"Sounds good to me." He flashed her a smile that woke up something cold and wounded inside her. Something she wasn't sure she was ready to deal with. Something that stole her breath and made her wish she was anything other than a tired surgeon at the end of a fourteen-hour procedure.

She covered her shock by stepping away to grab her purse.

They didn't talk on the way to the restaurant. She was tired and sore and none too happy with her reaction to him. Her last boyfriend had been an overprotective lawyer who seemed content with her erratic schedule, at least at first. He liked it when she came home physically tired and emotionally exhausted. At first. Eventually, he came to resent the amount of time she put in at the hospital. Complaining louder and louder that he wasn't a priority in her life. She didn't care about their relationship. She was too busy being a surgeon to be a partner. Blah, blah, blah.

This detective seemed quite happy to walk without chatter. It wasn't until they'd put in their orders that he said anything at all about why he'd sought her out.

"Your father is Arthur Stoneman?" he asked in a careful tone that made her stomach clench in fearful anticipation.

"Yes." She hadn't seen her dad in over a year. What had he done that would bring a detective to talk to her at this hour?

"Vietnam veteran?"

"Yes." The familiar cloak of guilt hung itself around her neck. "And before you ask, yes, I knew he was homeless. I tried to help him with rent, but he walked away from the last place and refused to take any money from me." She sucked in a breath to go on, to explain that no matter what she did her father believed he *belonged* on the street. "We argued. He left angry. I haven't seen him in a long time."

"I get it," the detective interrupted. "It happens to a lot of vets."

She was too tired for this. "What, *exactly*, happens? I tried to reason with him, but nothing I said made a difference."

"Post-traumatic stress."

That didn't explain anything. Not really. "There are a whole host of stress disorders. How does having one make a man *want* to live homeless?"

"For a lot of soldiers PTSD takes away the ability to feel safe anywhere. They begin living like they did out in the field. Constantly moving, always on guard, trusting no one." George leaned forward and lowered his voice until it rumbled across the space between them like thunder before a storm. "Imagine being trained to live off the land and blend in with your surroundings while watching for an enemy who will try his best, his *very best*, to kill you. *If* you don't kill him first."

His words locked her throat, making it hard to breathe. The last time she'd seen her father he'd been wearing dirty clothes, had lost weight, and looked like he hadn't slept in days. It was an image she couldn't get out of her head. "That's awful."

"That's life in and after the service for many."

His gaze reflected the nightmare he described, and she *knew*. "You're a veteran, too."

It wasn't a question, but he answered it anyway with a short nod. "Iraq and Afghanistan." He pulled in a deep breath through his nose, like he was mentally regrouping, blinked and leaned back. "My father was a Vietnam vet, too, so I'm familiar with the situation from both sides of the fence."

"I understand." He'd just given her the insight into her father's behavior she'd needed for years. "Thank you. This explains so much." Emotions rushed through her—relief, understanding, regret, and a renewed sense of hope. Enough to make her giddy. "Has he been arrested? Is that why you wanted to talk to me?"

His body stilled, his face draining of color until it resembled granite, complete with fissures. "No." His lips tightened, flattened out. "Your father was murdered a few hours ago."

Allison couldn't have heard him correctly. "What?"

"I'm very sorry for your loss." The detective's voice sounded so far away.

"No." She shook her head. "No, that's not..." Hard, harsh breathing was all she could hear. It took her a moment to realize it was her own.

Her fingers opened and closed convulsively, reaching for hands she'd never hold again. The detective slid his large palms and long fingers over hers and she latched on to them like they were her lifeline.

Her mind flitted from one thought to another, memories of her father from various times in her life, without direction or control, until one word rose to the surface. "Murdered?"

"He was shot. Close range." The detective's words were cool and clipped, but his hands were warm as they held hers, his thumbs stroking over the pulse points on both wrists as if coaxing her to stay in the here and now. "Did he ever mention anyone who might be angry with him, someone with an ax to grind?"

She shook her head, hoping to hide her grief and confusion. "No. He was never one to complain, and he never talked about the past. It was as if it didn't exist for him." All the fun times when she was a kid, vacations, Christmases, birthdays, he didn't want to talk about any of it. Wouldn't even go to a family reunion. It had hurt her in ways she hadn't suspected until long after he had disappeared into the human fog of Chicago's streets.

"It was probably all that existed for him, and he didn't want to burden you with it. Men with his sort of courage, his selflessness, never do." The detective sounded tired, sad, and unsurprised.

"What do you mean, his sort of courage? Did you know him?"

"No, but I read his record and his citation. He was the rare type of man who really did put everyone else first."

"You're talking about his military record?"

"Yes." George Eaglefeather stared at her for a long moment then added, "And his Medal of Honor."

Allison must have heard wrong. "What Medal of Honor?"

George let out a huge sigh. "He never told you?"

Her father had won the *Medal of Honor*? "No." She laughed and cried at the same time, more than a little hysterical. "He didn't." Tears rolled down her face and dripped off her nose.

"Damn." George slid out of his side of the booth and into hers, wrapped his long arms around her, and coaxed her head onto his shoulder. She latched on to him and let her grief take her under.

She never cried. Certainly not in public and never, *ever* on a man she'd just met. Somehow their food had arrived while she was crying, without her noticing.

She *did* notice something else, though. George was whispering words of comfort in her ear, holding her like she was precious and fragile. Like she mattered to him. No man had made her feel that way in years.

Her arms were around his neck, she was halfway onto his lap, and she'd gotten the front of his shirt wet from all her crying. Well, no wonder he held her like she was china. He was probably trying to figure out how to get the hysterical woman out of the restaurant and into an ER for a Valium.

Allison pulled away slightly, let herself suck in and breathe out one more big lungful of air, then glanced up at him and said, "Sorry. I'm not usually this—damp." She couldn't remember the last time she'd cried like this. Medical school had taught her more than how to heal—it had also taught her how to box up any unwanted emotions. Somewhere along the way, that evolved into *all* her emotions. All of them neatly stacked away in the back of her brain. Until today. A bulldozer had ripped through the boxes tearing them open, letting loose every nightmare and monster she'd ever battled.

A slow smile transformed his face from one of attractive concern to handsome sinner. "S'okay. I'm an air-dry kind of guy." He let that smile light up the place for another second or two before putting it away like the concealed weapon it was. "Feeling better?"

"Yeah. Embarrassed, but not so shocky."

"It'll come and go, that feeling, so don't be surprised if you feel...*damp* again tomorrow."

A blush stole over his face and he pulled his plate over and began eating like he'd been stung by a Taser.

Okay, so maybe she wasn't the only one feeling embarrassed.

Once she had a bite of food, her stomach took over and she ate like she hadn't had anything in weeks.

"So," she said as she chased the syrup on her plate with a piece of pancake. Her hand shook and she stared at it. *That would never do.* She found her professional mental mask and slipped it over her features. "How did you find me so fast?"

"Your dad handed me a paper bag with a bunch of newspaper clippings in it. All the stories were about you. Some of them went back ten years." He reached into his pocket and pulled out something. "This was in the bag, too." He placed a blue tiger's eye pendant on the table.

"I've never seen this before." She ran a finger down the center of the stone, following the eye pattern.

"He must have wanted you to have it," George said.

She turned the pendant over. The stone seemed ordinary enough, nothing expensive or rare. As she turned it in her hands, the overhead lights reflected off the stone and she saw what made this stone special.

"It's the color of my eyes." She glanced up at George and held his gaze. "See?"

He looked at her for a long time. "Yeah." His voice sounded unused and raspy. "They're something else."

"My dad always said I had a tiger's eyes," she said, smiling at the memory. "He said that, a hundred years ago, I'd have been an important woman."

"You *are* an important woman."

She smiled at his affronted tone. "I meant among our people. I'm Lakota Sioux. Well, three-quarters, anyway."

"I'm half. On my father's side. Irish on my mother's."

"Irish and Sioux. Wow, that's some kind of stubborn combination."

He chuckled. "You don't want to know what my ex-wife called it."

Allison snorted. "If she walked away from you, she's an idiot and her opinion doesn't matter."

He stared at her with his mouth hanging open. *Holy shit.* Did that just come out of her mouth?

"I mean…" What was she doing? What was she saying? Her father had just been *murdered*. She stood on an emotional precipice and it was sucking her in. "I think I'm doing the *damp* thing again."

***

George was certain he was doing the *damp* thing, too. He didn't have her excuse, though. All he had was the feeling of being whacked on the back of the head with an emotional two-by-four. From staring into her eyes.

He'd never seen anything more beautiful than her blue-and-amber eyes.

She ducked her head and chewed on her bottom lip. Anxious. Embarrassed. Scared.

Nope. Not on his watch. Not where she was concerned. Her father couldn't protect her anymore, but he could. He could honor the man who gave so much of himself to others that he'd lost everything.

"Hey," he said, trying to catch her amazing gaze again. "Don't...hide from me. You and I, we're good."

She flicked a glance at him, her cheeks a rosy pink. "Are we?"

"Yeah. This is an odd conversation containing some pretty shitty news. I think we're both allowed some leeway regarding whatever comes out of our mouths."

She straightened, then nodded. "Thank you." She glanced at their empty plates. "What's next?"

Keep digging, that's what. He had to admire her tenacity. She wasn't giving in to grief, but keeping her focus on the problem at hand—but this kind of loss was powerful and insidious. "Has anyone talked to you recently about your dad?"

"No."

"Anyone phoning you, emailing you, or leaving messages?"

Her shoulders tightened up and the hair on the back of George's neck itched. "No one I know, but there have been several messages left on my work voice mail from a man. He never leaves his name, just a number. He says it's important, but never says why. I've never called him back."

He pulled out a small notebook and a pencil. "How many messages?"

She shrugged. "Maybe four or five?"

"When was the first one?"

She glanced at the ceiling, thinking. "A while ago. Maybe three months?"

"At home or at work?"

"Oh, only at work. My personal cell phone number is not one I give out."

"Good. Don't. Do you have any of these messages saved?"

"No, but I did write down the number." She grabbed her purse and started pulling things out until a pile of stuff sat on the table. "Ah, here it is." She held out a crumpled piece of paper.

He noted the number in his notebook and phone. A local number. Interesting.

He glanced up and found her watching him with tired, red-rimmed eyes. "I've got a couple of other leads I need to follow, as well as this one. What's your cell phone number? I'd like to keep you in the loop."

Relief and gratitude put a shaky smile on her face.

Not quite the response he wanted. No, he wanted to see the stress gone and a smile on her face so he added in a sly tone, "You know, the one you *never* give out."

The wide-eyed blink she gave him would've made an owl proud. He could see the thoughts and emotions as they flitted over her features. Shock, confusion, and, finally, humor. She started to laugh and touched his arm.

There it was, the reaction he was looking for. The one that said she saw him as a man, and not just a cop.

He wanted her. Something about her touched his soul, reached out to him and whispered life's secrets. He'd never had a reaction like this to a woman. Instant and certain.

Slow down. He would take things easy, but he wasn't going to walk out of her life when this case was done.

"How about I escort you home." It should have been a question, but the only answer he was prepared to accept was *yes*, so why give her the idea that she could say *no*?

Her "Sure" was spoken between chuckles as he slid out of the booth and guided her out of the restaurant. He handed the waitress a few bills for their pancakes on the way out.

The temperature had dropped while they ate, and she walked closer to him with her arms around herself. He peeled off his suit jacket and put it over her shoulders. She smiled at him, then noticed his Beretta nine mil holstered under his left arm.

"I hope I didn't get your gun...damp."

One of the worst days of her life and she had enough backbone to be funny. George had to force himself not to put his arm around her shoulders, too.

They strolled toward the hospital, but when she would have veered off toward her own car, he shook his head and steered her toward his in the public parking lot.

"I need my car—"

"I'll have some follow-up questions for you," he interrupted. "I can take you to it tomorrow and touch base with you at the same time."

Her sidelong glance measured him in a way that had him wanting to puff out his chest. "Very efficient."

"It's either that or get nothing done," he drawled as they reached his car and he opened the passenger door for her. "What are your plans for tomorrow morning?"

"I'm supposed to see patients at about eight. I don't have any surgeries booked for tomorrow, but that could change..."

"Take some time off," he suggested in a soft tone. "Give yourself a chance to process all this."

"Okay." She swallowed and nodded. "Okay."

"Where do you live?"

"Oh, not far. About five minutes away." She gave directions until George was parked in her stall at a modern-looking condominium. He got out of the car when she did.

"You don't have to walk me up." She said it as if the idea that a man might show care and concern was foreign to her.

"Yes, I do."

She sighed. "Are you like this all the time?"

"Like what?"

"Overly protective."

"I'm a Sioux warrior and a cop. That sounds about right."

She stopped walking to look at him. "Are you?"

"Yes. My father taught me to track as a boy, to learn the patterns of movement made by both prey and predator. I use that knowledge every day." The streets of Chicago weren't the grasslands of his youth, but some things still translated to asphalt and cement.

"My grandfather was a medicine man," Allison said, chewing her bottom lip. "He taught me that the spirit and the body must be balanced for either to heal." She sounded almost...lost. "I think my father lost his balance a long time ago."

"And you?"

Her eyes were sad as she said, "Teetering on the edge, I think."

"Balance can be difficult to achieve and maintain alone."

She didn't reply, but that was okay. She would need time to think, time to let her memories out from wherever she'd hid them.

They climbed the stairs until they reached the third floor. She unlocked and opened her door, then turned to nod her head formally at him. "Thank you."

His gut tightened at her reserve. He'd allow it for now, but there was only so much distance he'd let her put between them. Something primal about her spoke to him, teased him, beckoned to him. He could no more ignore it than he could ignore his heritage. He gazed down at her and nodded back. "My pleasure. Call me if you need anything. I mean that." He'd visit her tomorrow. And the next day. Help her through the ridiculous amount of details involved in putting to rest a father who was also a murder victim.

"I will." The small smile on her face tantalized him. He'd like to see that expression on her face a lot more than the grief and sadness she carried now.

He waited until she closed and locked the door before making his way downstairs and to his car. He had his keys out when his cell phone rang.

It was Allison.

He reversed direction and ran as he answered. "What's wrong?"

"I found a letter on the floor inside my condo." Her voice was shaky. "I think you need to see it."

"I'll be there in ten seconds. Don't open the door until I get there." He ended the call and charged up the stairwell. He didn't slow until he reached her unit.

She must have been watching for him through the peephole because she threw the door open before he could knock. Her eyes were wide, her face pale, and her right hand shook. It held a single piece of paper.

She didn't immediately back away from the doorway, so he put his hands on her shoulders and gently guided her inside. He closed and locked the door. "Did you go into the bedroom or bathroom?"

"No. I headed for the kitchen to heat a kettle for tea and found this on the floor."

"Stay here," he ordered, pulling out his Beretta.

She gasped and staggered back a step.

"Don't go anywhere, okay?" he asked. "I want to be sure the rest of the condo is clear. That's all."

She nodded in a jerky movement that told him she was terrified. After everything that had happened, she would need some gentle handling.

He performed a quick but thorough search of her apartment and found no evidence that anyone was, or had been, inside. George returned to the entryway and looked at the bottom of the door.

"Do you think there's enough room for someone to have slid the envelope under it?"

"Yes. The pizza place down the street shoves menus under everyone's door at least once a week."

He glanced at the paper in her hand. "Did that come in an envelope or just like that?"

"There was an envelope, too." She held it out.

He nodded at the coffee table a few feet away. "The fewer people who handle it the better. Could you open the letter and spread it out for me?"

She did that, straightening then stepping away as soon as it was done, her shoulders dropping from their high, tight position.

The message was typed like a business letter with Allison's complete address in the upper-left corner, followed by today's date. There was no polite salutation, however, just a concise message:

He lied to everyone. It belongs to me. Leave it at the hospital's reception desk.

It was not signed.

"I have no idea what this *thing* is," she cried.

"It's something someone deemed important enough to murder your father for."

She jerked like he'd shot her in the chest. "What?" It came out as a harsh whisper. "What could be so important that it's worth more than a *man's life*?"

George sighed. He hated seeing her so bruised and battered by what this nutcase had done to her father, and now her. It made him want to gather her up and hold her so she could cry on his shoulder again. When he caught this guy, he was going to give him a lesson in how to treat other people the Sioux way. "I'm going to have to dig into your father's past a little to figure it out." He turned to face her. "Are you okay with that?"

"Yes." She closed her eyes briefly before staring at him as if he was the only safe thing in her universe. "Anything to stop this insanity."

She glanced around her home. "I can't believe he was right outside my door." She covered her mouth with one hand, her face pale and covered in a sheen of sweat.

That was it.

Time to get her in a location he *knew* was safe. "Pack a bag. Enough for a couple of days."

She frowned and blinked. "What?"

He gently took her hand and tugged her toward the bedroom he'd looked at earlier. "Throw some clothes and your toothbrush in a bag. You're not staying here tonight. Maybe not tomorrow night, either."

She trotted after him. "Where will I stay?"

This idea could get him fired, but fuck it. She needed him more than he needed his job. He could always move back to Wyoming. "My place."

***

Allison tried to process what George had said in that short, matter-of-fact way of his, but found it impossible to understand what he was saying. His place? *His place?* "Oh, but—"

"Can you see yourself sleeping here?" he asked, his tone as unyielding as stone.

"No." Okay, okay, he was right. Her hands fluttered around aimlessly and she stared at them like she'd never seen them before. Like they belonged to someone else.

George nudged her with one large shoulder. "Pack. Clothes. Bag."

Bag. Right, there was one in the closet. She pulled it out and put it on her bed.

Clothes. Work clothes?

She grabbed a set of scrubs, but George took them and put them back in her dresser. "No working. Not for a few days."

"But—"

"Look at yourself," he ordered in a surprisingly soft tone.

She glanced down. Her hands and knees were shaking like she was an alcoholic trying to dry out after a month long bender.

George put a pair of jeans on her outstretched hands. "Those fit?"

"I think so."

He opened another drawer and dropped a couple of shirts on top of the jeans. Next he found socks. When he opened her underwear drawer, he paused then said, "Maybe you should pick out whatever you need from this one."

She grabbed a couple items and shoved everything into the bag.

"Better bring some shampoo and soap, unless you want to smell like men's aftershave."

That almost made her laugh. How could she even think of laughing when her father had just been murdered and the murderer was now stalking her?

"Allison," George said, rubbing her arms like she was a child to be soothed. He sighed. "It's okay."

"No." She pulled away and paced, anger surging through her at the injustice of...everything. "It's not okay." She clenched her hands so hard it felt as if her bones would break.

"It's not," he agreed. "But we have to keep moving forward despite the horrible things people do to each other."

"Stop being reasonable."

"Uh, what should I do, then?"

"Scream? Throw things? Punch a pickpocket?"

"I usually go to the shooting range."

"The shooting range?" Guns, loud noises, and shooting bullets into targets. "Can we go right now?"

George gave her a half smile. "It's two in the morning. It's closed."

She deflated. "Damn. That sounded like...fun."

"You shouldn't say that to a cop. I might think you're flirting with me." He left the bathroom, that sexy half smile on his face.

He had to know how distracting it was, right?

Maybe that was the point.

Allison grabbed a few more things out of her bathroom, tossed everything into the bag, and headed to the door. Normally, her home was her refuge, but not now. Not after...tonight. The ugliness of the outside world had slipped in under the door and was now a resident. She couldn't face the loss of her sanctuary on top of everything else. "Please, can we go?"

He nodded and went out the door first, then waved at her to follow.

She hurried after him, sighing in relief as she got into his car. They were on their way before she thought to ask, "Do you live far?"

"About fifteen minutes." He glanced at her. "No roommate, wife, or kids. It's a one-bedroom apartment close to the office."

"The office, huh?"

He shrugged. "I'm trying to appear nonthreatening."

She nearly started laughing again, but managed to say with some sarcasm, "Nonthreatening. You? Never."

He shifted nervously. "I'm a big, mean-looking guy. Sometimes people get nervous around me. Uncomfortable even."

"The only people who are going to get nervous because you're..." she waved a hand in front of him, "...you, are criminals and idiots." She folded her arms across her chest and narrowed her gaze at him. "I'm neither. I find you reassuringly large and imposing. I'll sleep much better knowing you're close by."

"Good." There was a pleased, intensely masculine tone to his voice that should have made her nervous.

Was she so scared that she was willing to put herself in the hands of a stranger just because he appeared strong enough to defend her? Or was there something more?

Her head was too full and her heart too sore to try to figure it out. He was a detective who'd done everything he could to help and support her. She'd worry about the rest tomorrow, or the next day.

His apartment was sparsely furnished and looked almost too clean. No dishes in the sink or socks on the floor by the couch in the living room. Did anyone actually live here? She stood in front of the door and for the first time since she'd met him, didn't know what to say to Detective George Eaglefeather. *"Nice place. When was the last time you visited?"*

He looked at her, then glanced around his home and scratched his head. "I'm not here much. Just to sleep, mostly. There's a lady down the hall who comes in and cleans once a week whether the place needs it or not."

Wow, the guy could read minds, too? Nope. Not dealing with it. "Oh."

He sighed. "Come on." And trudged down the short hall and into another room. His bedroom.

She stared at the bed. A king. It took up almost all of the space. There was a scent here that had her muscles relaxing. Pine. Musk. Man.

George's scent.

"Good night." George's voice was abrupt.

She turned, but he was already gone, the door closed.

What the—?

Allison frowned at the door, then frowned at the bed. She grabbed her toothbrush and toothpaste and entered the bathroom across the hall. After brushing her teeth she went back into the bedroom and put on her fuzzy, cozy pajamas that made her look like a girl at a sleepover party.

Armed for a battle, she found George pretending to sleep on the couch. It was several inches too short for him to stretch out on.

"This is ridiculous."

He snored. Badly. Not even a three-year-old would believe it.

"George?"

He sighed, then said, "What?"

She was about to shock the shit out of him, but she didn't care. She was at her limit. "Will you sleep with me?"

He didn't answer right away. "Huh," he said with his eyes closed. "I thought I was still awake."

"You *are* awake."

He swung his feet onto the floor, scrubbed his face then stood and looked at her. "You want to repeat your last question?"

Crap, he was going to make this difficult. What could she say that would make sense? *Hey, big guy, I'm scared out of my mind and you're the only thing I trust right now?*

Huge hands grabbed hers and pulled them apart.

She glanced up at his solemn face.

"Your fingers are going to be sore if you keep pulling at them that hard."

"I'm not saying *anything* right. I wasn't asking..." Tears cooled her cheeks. Great, now she was crying. "You're *safe*."

"I'm not a teddy bear," he growled.

"I'm not a child," she snapped. Then she smacked him on the chest.

"You're..." he paused, "...a victim."

"Bullshit." Now that pissed her off. She wasn't weak, she was in shock. There was a big difference between the two. "I'm hurt, but I'm no victim."

His gaze weighed, measured, and the laugh lines next to his eyes told her he'd decided. "No victims here." He looked her up and down. "Ready for bed?"

She nodded in quick, sharp movements—worried he might change his mind—and rushed into the bedroom.

Before, the bed looked huge. Now, it seemed too small.

"Which side do you prefer?" she asked in a small voice.

"I usually sleep in the middle." He walked past her to lie down on the bed, close to the edge.

He looked much too good with his hands under his head, watching her with half-closed eyes. Desire curled through her body, followed by guilt, doubt, and a host of other muddled emotions.

No Sioux warrior *or* Chicago cop was going to want a woman as messed up as she was. She crawled up the bed, wiggled under the covers, and plunked her head on a pillow.

George extended one hand to her.

She looked at it for a moment, then slipped hers over it and soaked up the strength he offered. His scent—clean maleness—washed away all the fear, leaving only sorrow.

A sob escaped from a throat too tight with tears.

He wrapped her in impossibly long arms and pressed his lips to her hair.

Grief gripped her chest and shook her hard.

George whispered Sioux words of comfort, and they released the pent-up emotions swirling through her. She let herself weep until there was nothing left.

***

George held the woman in his arms as the storm she'd been holding inside burst out of her. He'd been expecting this, he just didn't know when.

He was going to get damp again.

He'd let her get him soaking wet if it made her feel better.

He hadn't wanted to get on a bed with her—she was too tempting a woman—but now that he was here, it was the right place. She needed him and, though she didn't know it, he needed her.

For a long time, he'd thought that being a cop and a warrior were mutually exclusive things. For once, they weren't. With her, he could be both. With her he didn't have to hide his Native American heritage.

It took a long time, but she eventually fell asleep.

Smart, beautiful, and stubborn, she probably had a list of eligible men interested in her.

George stared at the ceiling, uncertain about how to court a woman who appeared out of reach.

He was a half-breed Sioux, ex-military, homicide detective in the big city with no real home and nothing much to offer.

One problem at a time. First he had to solve a murder.

George closed his eyes, kissed her temple, and let sleep take him.

***

Allison woke alone. She frowned at the dent in the pillow next to hers. At least she hadn't imagined sleeping beside him.

She put her hand down to push herself up and something underneath it made a crinkled sound. A note.

Ali, I've gone in to work to stick my nose into things the murderer isn't going to like. Relax. Order pizza, and feel free to call me on my cell if you need anything.

She was on her own.

With a face covered in salty tear tracks and no answers to the question of why anyone would want to kill her father. Or what to do about a man she wanted far too much, who embodied everything she wanted. Choices, a career, freedom.

She thought she had those things while her father was alive, but she hadn't. She'd just found a different way to tie her hands. Responsibility, schedules, the needs of others.

George gave her choices, asked questions, and found answers.

A kind of freedom she'd never experienced before.

She showered, dressed, then wandered into George's kitchen to see if he had the makings for breakfast.

His fridge contained leftover Chinese food, a half loaf of bread, and a gallon of milk. No wonder he'd told her to order pizza.

She grabbed her cell phone and called him.

He answered on the first ring. "Feather."

"Stone," she replied in the same business-first tone.

"Have you eaten?" he asked. Business indeed. Where was the caring man from last night?

"No. I just took a look in the fridge. It's kind of bare."

"I'll swing by and pick you up. I've found out a couple of interesting things. We can talk while you eat."

He was there in less than five minutes. He took her to a small café that boasted the best soup in the city. While she ate hers, George opened a file containing several photos and papers.

"This is your dad in uniform." George showed her the formal photo of her father from when he was in the Army.

She was amazed at how strong he looked, how confident. What had happened to him?

"This," George said, pulling out a group shot, "is your dad's unit. See this guy?" He pointed at another man. "He was often paired up with your dad. His name was Tony Lacosta. Tony was one of seven men your father saved when they inadvertently attacked a bunch of Vietnamese dug in and shooting the shit out of them. Only, Tony tried to take the credit."

"What?" Anger, sorrow, and guilt built up inside her and she didn't know what to do or how to feel anymore.

"Here's the official report from your dad's commanding officer, along with the signed statements from the rest of the men and the official citation request." George showed her more papers. "It looks like Tony not only tried to take credit for the lives saved, he tried to say your dad didn't do a damn thing. Everyone else contradicted him."

"Is he the man who killed my father?" She *needed* to know.

"No. He died last year. His son, however, filed an official protest regarding the awarding of the Medal of Honor to your dad. He was unsuccessful. He does have a handgun registered to him of the same caliber as the bullets that killed your dad. I'm bringing him in as a person of interest."

"Why would someone claim to be a hero when there were witnesses to say he wasn't?"

"I don't know. I do have a friend who's still in the military. He's in recruitment, but he knew your dad. He might be able to give us information that's not on any form." He waved his hands over the papers in front of him.

Maybe he could give her some insight on why her father had made the choices he had. "Okay, let's go talk to him."

"I talked to him this morning. He's on his way here."

"Really? So soon?"

"The Army takes a dim view of people who murder their veterans, especially Medal of Honor recipients." George pulled out the unit picture again. "See this guy, here on the end?" He pointed at the soldier.

"Yes." She leaned closer to get a better look. His strong jaw and stern gaze caught her attention. "Wow, he looks just like you."

George's tone was deep and strong. "That's 'cause he's *my* father."

Allison stared at George with her mouth open. "You...I...our fathers served in the same unit?"

"Yeah. The Army tended to stick several Native Americans in the long-range patrol units, with only a few white men to make things look good to the paper pushers. I recognized your last name when I heard it yesterday, but couldn't remember where until I saw the unit photo. I have the same picture in a drawer at home." He took a sip of coffee. "My dad used to tell stories about 'Nam. He never talked about combat much, but he did talk about the best tracker in the unit. Stoneman could track a ghost, Dad said. He even learned a thing or two from your father."

"Wow. I wish I had known." Tears prickled her eyes again. "That's amazing, and sad that we had this connection and didn't know until now."

George nodded and shared his sorrow-filled gaze with her for a few seconds.

A buzzing noise had him checking his phone. "Murphy is ten minutes away. Let's go."

She tried to pay the bill, but the woman at the cash register refused to accept her money. "What's with that?" she asked George as they left.

"I eat here every day. I have a tab."

"And, what, a woman isn't allowed to pay for her coffee?"

He shrugged. "I'm an old-fashioned guy."

Yes, he was, and she found she liked that very much.

As they headed across the street toward the police station, George's phone buzzed again.

George listened then ended the call and said to her, "Our person of interest is in the wind."

Two men—one who might be able to tell her things about her father she didn't know, and one who might have murdered him—and she was about to come face-to-face with one of them.

Her pace slowed. Did she want to hear what he had to say? She'd already learned that her father had kept secrets from her. How much worse might they get?

"Allison?" His tone softened. "Ali?"

Her head jerked up at her nickname. Damn it, she'd stopped walking and George was looking at her like she was doing something ridiculous. "Sorry. I'm just—"

"Thinking too hard," George interrupted. He strode back to her and took her hand. "You're the observer today. You don't have to talk to anyone." He squeezed her fingers. "You're not alone."

She took in a breath to calm her nerves. "Okay." She could do this. She *had* to do this. "Okay."

They walked into the building and made their way through to George's desk. It was one of several in a large open-concept office space. A man in an Army uniform sat in a chair next to a desk. As soon as he saw them coming toward him, he got to his feet and extended his hand toward George.

"Good to see you, Feather."

"Likewise, Meathead."

"Meathead?" Allison snapped her jaw shut. She hadn't even been introduced to the guy and she was already asking questions.

"The name I was christened with on day one of basic training," the tall, broad soldier told her with a polite smile. His hair was clipped short so that the top of his head looked perfectly flat. "I also answer to Murphy."

She looked at George. "Yours was Feather?"

"Could've been worse," he said with a crooked grin. He nodded at his friend. "Have a seat." He grabbed another chair from the next desk over and gestured for her to sit in it.

"This is Allison Stoneman, Art's daughter," George said to Murphy with a level of pride that made her sit up straighter. "Since I talked to you yesterday, a letter was left for Ali at her apartment. It references the murder and demands the return of something of value. The only person who had an issue with Art was Tony Lacosta, but Lacosta is dead."

"He might be gone, but his claim that he should have won the medal given to Stoneman isn't. Lacosta's son, Marcus, has filed enough paperwork to fill a cabinet regarding the medal."

"Has he got a case?" George asked.

"No. It's been investigated three times now. Art Stoneman advanced toward an entrenched enemy position, taking three bullets in the process, two in the chest and one in his left leg. His actions allowed seven other soldiers, including Lacosta, to retreat to a safer position."

"Three bullets?" Allison asked, barely able to get the words out. "Two in the chest? How did he survive those kinds of injuries?"

"Ma'am," Murphy began, leaning toward her slightly. "He was damn lucky and he was a stubborn son of a...gun. He lost a lot of blood, but he didn't lie down and die. He kept moving, covering his unit's six, and was able to get extracted along with the rest."

"Six?" The courage it took to do it, the fear he must have felt and overcome...was overwhelming.

George leaned in close and said, "He kept covering their retreat, keeping himself in the line of fire."

"Even after being shot three times?" The selflessness of what he'd done, the depth of caring and character it took to put other people before himself, put the last years of her father's life in a new light.

George nodded. "Now you know why he was awarded the medal."

She grabbed George's hand. "He said he wouldn't live with me or take money from me because it was for my protection." She stopped to swallow the sorrow blocking her throat. "I thought he was paranoid. Seeing conspiracies where there weren't any. He told me to be careful, to be sure no one followed me."

"The third and last investigation uncovered new information regarding the incident. One of the men your father saved had a diary that didn't come to light until after his death. He recorded a very detailed account of the event, and it placed the blame for stumbling onto that nest of enemy soldiers squarely on Lacosta's shoulders. He'd led them in the wrong direction, even after your dad tried to correct him."

"Oh my God." Why would the man who'd caused the situation claim to have saved the day?

"When I informed his son of this, he refused to believe it. Claimed I—and the Army—was lying to protect Stoneman, who was the real culprit. He became verbally and physically belligerent. I had to have him escorted out."

"How belligerent?" George's voice was soft, but there was a thread of steel in it that made Allison shiver.

"As soon as he heard something he didn't like, he stopped listening and started threatening everything from a law suit to..." Murphy paused as if searching for the right word. "Violence."

One of George's eyebrows rose. "Did you write it up?"

Murphy tapped a manila envelope on George's desk. "Brought you a copy."

The two men continued to talk about the report, but Allison stopped listening. Lacosta might be the most logical suspect in her father's murder, but she was just as guilty. She should have insisted he stay with her or in an apartment or somewhere safe. She should have kept asking, kept checking on him. She should have done *something*.

Instead, she'd allowed him to convince her he was making reasonable decisions for himself. That he was okay.

She'd been so *stupid*.

"Ali?"

Her name, spoken in George's deep, smooth voice, tugged her out of the negative feedback loop she'd put her thoughts in. "Yes? What?"

"I have to leave," Murphy said, getting to his feet. He held out his hand and shook hers with surprising gentleness. "I'm deeply sorry for your loss. If you need *anything*, please call me."

Damn these strong men and their vows of service. She was going to cry again. *Suck it up, princess. No more crying until you've faced the man who killed your dad.* She forced her bottom lip to stop quivering. "Thank you." She watched him leave, then turned to find George looking at her with eyes that saw far too much.

"He left his card for you." George held it out to her.

She took it and put it in her purse. "Thanks."

George didn't look away from her face. "You okay?"

"Is it bad of me to hope I *never* have a reason to call him?"

He pursed his lips, considering, then said, "Nope."

"George," she said with a sigh. "I'd laugh if I didn't feel like crying so much."

"That's probably not going to change anytime soon," he said, gesturing at her to follow him. "I've got something to show you."

Whatever it was, she didn't want it. She was too tired to deal with anything.

George took her down a couple of floors to a desk where he had to sign in. They entered a small office. "Wait here for a minute."

He was gone before she could reply.

When he came back, he had a small box in his hands. He set it on the table in front of her and opened it.

She stared at the object inside for several seconds before she realized what it was. "This is his medal?"

"Yeah. He was wearing it under his clothes. We've processed it for trace evidence, so once the case is closed you can take it home."

The medal lay on the bottom of the box—the blue ribbon which would have gone around her father's neck stained with dirt and sweat.

She reverently touched one of the points on the scratched and discolored star. "It looks like it went through a war."

"It did."

More than one. The second war so deceptive she hadn't even realized it was happening. Not in a foreign land thousands of miles away, but here at home, in America. All around her. A silent war all veterans fought, only the enemy was themselves. She'd been blind to it, hadn't wanted to see it, and so she didn't. The price for her ignorance had been too high. "It's my fault."

He frowned. "What?"

"I should have done more. Argued longer. Insisted he stay with me or somewhere safe." Breathing hard, she struggled to find enough air in the room to fill her lungs. *"It's my fault."*

"No." George's voice was harder than any stone. "Your father was murdered. You did everything you could, but some men—" He stopped, then continued in a quieter tone. "Some men don't know how to accept help, even when their lives depend on it."

His gaze—tired, so very *tired*—told her he knew more about that than he might want to admit.

"You've seen this before?"

"Too many times. Too many times in my own head. My mother once told me that the *y* chromosome had a special stupid section. I think she might be right."

That wasn't what she expected him to say. "You're an honest man."

"Everyone has at least one vice."

"If honesty is your vice, I'd hate to discover what your virtues are."

"I don't have any." His voice had lost all its vitality, all its warmth.

She didn't reply except to arch a brow.

"Ready to go?" he asked as if their conversation hadn't injured him in the slightest. But she knew it had.

Just like a man to stop talking at the good part.

She glanced down at the box and its contents. "No." She looked around. It was safe here, full of men who'd chosen to serve and protect, but she'd have to face the real world sometime. "But it doesn't matter. I *need* to go." She closed the lid, put the box back on the table, and stood.

He led the way out of the room and back up to the main floor. "I'm going to walk you back to my place, where you're going to take a nap. When I'm done work, we'll do takeout."

It sounded so normal, but nothing *felt* normal anymore. Still, she couldn't let him get away with ordering her around. "I'm not a five-year-old. You can't make me have a nap."

"When was the last time you let anyone take care of you?"

"When I was five years old."

He snorted and opened the front door of the building for her. "Stubborn."

"I prefer the word *persistent*." She walked down the cement stairs to the sidewalk then stopped to take in a breath of fresh air. "Though, right now all I feel is...uncertain and numb."

George stood next to her with his hands in his pockets. "Grief is a long trail, but you don't have to travel it alone."

His gaze told her he meant every word. "You don't even know me."

"I know everything I need to know." He took a step closer to her, then another. "You're a strong, caring woman who gives of herself to others without reservation, without thought to her own well-being."

"But—"

His hand caressing her face stopped her from saying more. So gentle. "If you truly don't want me, say so now."

She couldn't say a word. She did want him, but did she deserve him?

He smiled and leaned toward her until his lips were only inches away from hers. "We'll go slow." His head lowered and she tilted her chin to better reach him.

"Allison Stoneman," demanded an angry voice.

She jerked away from George, but he thrust her behind him before she could see who it was.

"That's close enough." George's voice was a hard command.

"She has something that belongs to me." The man stepped to the side to make eye contact with her.

Was this the man who killed her father? She'd imagined a big man who exuded danger and threat. The man before her didn't. Of average height, he appeared no more than middle-aged and had a receding hairline. He resembled her accountant.

"Where is it?" he asked, his voice so cold it quivered.

"Who are you?" she asked.

He all but spat out his answer. "The son of the man your father disgraced."

That's when she noticed he held a handgun in his right hand. It was pointed at the ground, but that didn't make her feel any safer.

Did he kill her father with that gun?

"Mr. Lacosta," George said in a calm voice. "Why don't we go inside and discuss the item you believe you're entitled to?"

Two uniformed police officers came out of the station and moved toward the man with the gun, but George waved at them to stop and they paused.

"No discussion," Lacosta said, taking a step forward. "It belongs to me."

Allison slid away from George's protection. "Did you shoot my father?" The words were out of her mouth before she realized she said them.

Lacosta sneered. "He deserved what he got. He lied and took all the glory that should have been my father's. He stole my father's medal and the life my father should have had."

"Life?" she demanded. "*Life?* You mean the one where he lived on the streets, too frightened of bringing the bogeyman home with him? No," Allison told him with a shake of her head. For the first time since she'd seen George in the hall outside the OR, she felt strong and unafraid. "You're mistaken. *Your* father is the one who lied. I've seen the proof."

Lacosta let out a cross between a growl and a scream as he raised the gun and pointed it at her.

George stepped in front of her as a shot rang out.

Time slowed, turning seconds into minutes.

George stumbled back and she lunged forward to catch him. He was big and heavy, and he dragged her to the sidewalk as he fell. Blood coated the front of his chest on the left side. He took in a breath and his chest gurgled and whistled.

Goddamn.

Movement out of the corner of her eye had her glancing up in time to see the uniformed police officers shoot Lacosta twice. His body collapsed to the ground like a rag doll.

Was he dead?

Was it really over?

Lacosta's body was still, his chest motionless.

Perhaps now her father's spirit would be at peace.

Time returned to normal and Allison put aside her grief to don her surgeon's mask.

"I need an ambulance," she called out.

She eased George onto his back and began pulling open his suit jacket and shirt. Fabric tore and buttons flew, but she didn't slow down. The bullet had entered a couple of inches below his collarbone and the wound made bubbling noises with each breath he took.

More police came running out of the station. "I need gloves," she yelled at them.

Someone thrust a pair under her nose and she grabbed one and smacked it over the holes in George's chest.

"Is an ambulance on the way?" she asked the crowd of uniformed men.

"Should be here in two minutes," one said, kneeling next to her. "I'll take over until the paramedics get here." He gave her an odd sort of dismissive smile.

"Why would you do that? *I'll* be taking this man into surgery as soon as we get him to the hospital."

The cop's jaw dropped. "You're a doctor?"

"Thoracic surgeon," she said absently, noting the signs of blood loss on George's face—pale skin, blue around his lips. "Prop up his legs for me." She got in his line of sight. "Are you with me, George?"

"Try...and get...rid of...me," he said slowly, gasping for air between every word.

"You can stay as close to me as you like for as long as you like." She'd never said that to a patient or even a friend before.

"Promise?"

She made her voice a vow. "Absolutely."

*****

She'd given her word.

It was the first conscious thought George had as he swam against a heavy current trying to pull him under. But he'd been under long enough. He needed air now.

He needed Ali.

The ceiling above him was white and a machine beeped behind his head. He lifted his right arm and discovered an IV in the back of his hand, the tube filled with blood connected to a bag of it hanging next to his bed.

His other hand had an IV in it, too, but this one had a clear fluid in it.

He tried to sit up and found he couldn't. His fingers searched for a call button. Didn't all hospital beds have those?

"George, I'm here. It's okay."

There she was, dressed in surgical scrubs and wearing a paper hat. He'd never seen a more beautiful woman.

He smiled. "How am I doing?"

"Pretty good for a guy who had two bullets puncture one of his lungs and some significant internal bleeding." She said it matter-of-factly, but her face told a different story. There was fear in her eyes, but hope on her lips.

"Am I going to live?" His voice sounded strange to his ears, like he hadn't used it in years.

"I think so, as long as you follow all your doctor's instructions." Now he could see how much it cost her to be the one who operated on him. How difficult it had been for her to divorce her emotions.

He needed to soothe her, care for her, if not with the strength of his hands, then with the strength of his spirit. "Do you think she'll be unreasonable about those instructions?"

"Depends. She wants to take a personal interest in your recovery. A *very* close personal interest."

"That's a time saver."

"Oh?"

"It saves me from having to camp out in front of your door."

"Right now, you couldn't hold down a feather." She fussed with the blanket covering him.

He reached out, captured her wrist, and slowly pulled her closer. "You've had *this* feather in the palm of your hand since the moment I met you. Don't let me go."

"Never," she breathed, her lips coming to rest on his.

Their kiss was tender, a slow exploration of two people who knew they'd finally found the person who could complete them.

"My father," she said, her breathing fast and erratic, "would have liked you, would have welcomed you."

"You," George said, stroking her face with a shaking hand, "are the home I've been searching for. I love you."

Tears rolled down her face. Now she could cry. Now she could let herself heal. *Goodbye, Father. Thank you for leading me to this man.*

She smiled and kissed George again. "I love you, too."

Epilogue

Ten days later...

George glanced at the wheelchair the nurse brought in and dismissed it. There was no way he was going to let this twenty something girl push him around in it.

He slid off the hospital bed where he'd been waiting politely for his discharge to be completed and headed for the hallway.

"Mr. Eaglefeather, you're required to use the wheelchair after discharge," the nurse said, chasing after him and snagging his arm before he could make a clean getaway.

He glanced at her, her hand, then the chair and shrugged. "Go ahead and bring it if it makes you happy. I'm not riding in it."

"But—"

"I've got this, Maureen."

He froze, all his senses on alert as Allison's smooth contralto washed over him. For the last ten days they'd maintained a polite doctor/patient relationship, and he couldn't take one more second of it. He wanted nothing more than to throw her over his shoulder and take her out of this sterile place and into his own territory.

He'd strip them both to the skin and he'd love her so thoroughly and often she'd never think to treat him with polite concern ever again. He wanted all of her. Her passion and need, and as out of control as he was.

He'd been in the hospital for a week, recovering from the bullet wound that caused his lung to collapse and subsequent surgery. Surgery she'd performed. They hadn't had much of a chance to talk, none at all in private, and he had a few things he wanted to make clear to her.

He wanted her in his life.

As partner and lover.

He'd wait for however long it would take for her to become comfortable with the situation, but he wasn't going to back off like a civilized pansy ass.

He also hadn't counted on her coming armed. With a smile. "In the chair, hot shot."

"It's not dignified," he told her, allowing his displeasure with the situation to color his tone.

"The chair doesn't care who you are." She flashed that completely unfair smile again then took his arm and led him back to the offensive seat.

He allowed her to seat him in it, only because it was her, then she pushed him toward the elevator.

He sighed. "I feel like the pope or something."

"His chair is much fancier than this one," she said with only a slight smile on her face.

She wheeled him outside to a waiting Mercedes.

"Whose vehicle is this?" he asked as he was finally able to get out of the chair and leave it behind.

"Mine," she told him. The door locks snapped open and he slid into the passenger seat. He took in the leather seats and top of the line accessories, a lot more than a cop could afford. She drove them away from the hospital with the same competence he imagined she demonstrated with a scalpel.

She pulled up outside his building and even found an open stall in the tiny visitor parking area.

"You're coming up?" he asked, afraid that she might have changed her mind since she'd agreed they needed to talk in private.

She answered by following him into the building then into his apartment. Relief made him light-headed, but he managed not to act like a love sick fool.

He dropped the small satchel of personal items she'd collected and brought to the hospital for him and turned to her.

She was already moving, sliding into his embrace like she'd never left it. She held him tight, almost as tight as he held her.

Thank God.

They stood in front of his door, holding each other for several seconds before he realized she was shaking.

Shaking because she was crying.

She buried her head in the crook of his shoulder and he stroked her back as she released the tears he reckoned she'd held inside since he'd gotten shot.

After a few minutes she lifted her head, wiped her eyes and nose with the sleeve of her shirt then looked him square in the eye and said, "Don't you stand in front of a bullet meant for me ever again."

He cupped her face with one hand. "Sweetheart, there's no way I could ever make a promise like that. You're mine to protect." He kissed her. "Mine to cherish." Another kiss. "Mine to love."

She stared at him, her teeth set, eyes furious. "Stupid, stubborn..." She sucked in a breath. "And mine."

This time she kissed him. It was no sweet, gentle slide. Rather, it was hard, deep and shockingly dirty.

He loved it.

His hands found their way to cradle the back of her head, then one went south to cup her ass, hauling her in so he could press his erection against the softness of her belly.

They both groaned at the contact.

"Honey," he said, pulling back a little. "Slow down."

"Why?" she countered, kissing, licking and sucking his neck.

"I want to savor this," he hissed as she found his earlobe and nibbled on it. "Holy Christ."

"I *am* savoring," she told him, attacking his poor ear relentlessly. "And I plan on savoring over and over again."

He groaned and surrendered the win to his medicine woman.

He maneuvered her into his bedroom and onto his bed without tripping or falling. His hands couldn't stay in one place, roamed her body, trying to learn what she liked.

Her breasts filled his palms, her nipples tight points he couldn't wait to taste.

He slid one hand up her shirt to mold and tease her.

She moaned and arched into his hand.

He tugged her shirt up under her arms then pulled the cups of her bra down so he could feast on her.

She made an urgent sound and pressed his head to her.

She *liked* that.

He set himself the task of driving her out of her mind, moving from one breast to the other, devouring her with voracious hunger.

"Get this off me," she demanded, pushing at his shoulders. "Take your clothes off."

He didn't want to stop touching her, but naked sounded really good. He helped her get out of her shirt, then fought with his own, ignoring the painful twinges from his wound, while he watched her take off the bra.

Her breasts were full and her tight nipples called to him.

He got off the bed to strip off his pants and underwear, and groaned when she slithered out of hers. She didn't lay back and wait for him. She knelt on his bed, her gaze devouring his body, spending an ego-raising amount of time on his cock. "Come here."

He grinned. "Yes, ma'am." He climbed on the bed and reached for her, but before he could get his hands on her, she palmed his cock, and the pleasure of her touch held him hostage.

He shouted, his whole body going rigid as he turned every ounce of his will to not orgasm in her hand. He wanted to be inside her for that.

When he could move again, he glanced down and darn near came from the rapt expression on her face as she stroked him.

He took her hand off him and put it on his shoulder instead, only a few inches away from his bandaged wound. "That is something you shouldn't be playing with," he growled.

"Oh, but I just got started," she said, biting her bottom lip. "I was enjoying myself."

"I did too, a little too much. I," he said cradling one breast while he bore her down onto her back. "don't want to rush this." He pinched her nipple and she gasped.

He kissed her, long, slow and deep while he petted her, worshiped her with his hands.

"There's something to be said about a little speed," she panted in his ear.

"Hmm." Her neck was soft silk under his tongue.

"I—"

Whatever she'd been about to say was cut off by a gasp when he circled the opening to her body with one finger. When he slid down to suck and nibble on her nipples while he teased her, she arched under him and shivered.

He thrust his index finger into her wet heat and she grabbed hold of his short hair and pulled his head up. "Don't tease. I need you."

He grinned. "Yes, ma'am."

She blinked wide eyes at him. "You like it when I order you around?"

"Pleasing my woman is always at the top of my priority list." Then he leaned down and used his tongue on her clit.

She moaned and threw her head back.

She was earth and sky.

Freedom and family.

Love and life.

Life.

Desire and need shot through him so hard, he couldn't wait any longer to bring them together. He crawled up her body and made room for himself between her thighs.

She shook her head and rose, pushing him with firm hands so he was the one on his back. She straddled him and tried to sink onto him, but he wanted to tease her just a little more.

He took himself in hand, wetting the head of his cock by rimming it around her sensitive entrance to her body, she said, "Oh, thank God." And sank onto him.

He pushed inside at the same time, her slick channel hot and wet. Pleasure, so intense it set fire to every nerve in his body, rolled through him and he found himself teetering on the edge of his control.

He managed to retain enough restraint to let her rock against him until he was all the way in. "Ali?" his voice, low and rough, was barely recognizable as his own.

"You," she panted. "Fill me up." She rotated her hips and he lost it.

He lifted her up, pulled almost all the way out, then powered back in. It was perfect. She was perfect.

He set a steadily increasing pace after that, driving them both to the edge of orgasm.

"Please," she cried. "Just a little faster.

He had no intention of ignoring her request. He drove into her, hard and fast, and she screamed as her orgasm overtook her.

His own followed on the next thrust.

When he came down from the high, he kissed her leisurely. Wallowing in the knowledge she was his.

After a minute or two, he moved to pull out of her, but she clutched him close.

"Don't leave me," she whispered.

He smiled and kissed her again. "I will never leave you. You're my home."

Tears rolled down her face as she laughed. "And you're mine."

"Good, because this broken down old warrior has been looking for home for a long time."

Book Four
To Love & Honor

***

College sweethearts, Drew and Davina thought they'd be together forever, but after Davina catches Drew in a shower with a naked girl, she runs as far and as fast as she can. Angry with her for not trusting him, Drew tries to date other girls, but realizes too late that Davina is it for him. When a friend's wedding gives Drew the chance to apologize and make things right, he shows up at her door with his hat in his hand. Davina opens her hotel room door expecting to see her college roommate on the eve of her wedding, not Drew babbling about a misunderstanding and starting over. She finally gives him the response he deserves for breaking her heart, a bloody nose. Drew's not giving up. He intends to show her he's her man, no matter how long it takes or how long he has to grovel. Davina is worth it.

***

To Love & Honor

Moose Creek, Maine, hadn't changed a bit.

Davina Hobbs drove through the small town and noted the same businesses lining the main street as six years ago. The drug and grocery store, drive-in diner and barber shop.

The only thing that was different was the name of the county sheriff, Drew Cavendish.

Which was why she drove through town making sure to keep under the speed limit. Getting pulled over by Sheriff Cavendish was not an experience she wanted on this little pleasure trip.

She'd been to Moose Creek only once with her then boyfriend, the same Drew Cavendish. She'd been so in love with him, so certain they would make it.

Until the day she caught him with a naked girl in his shower.

It still hurt to think about it. The shame and embarrassment at discovering he was just like all his football-playing friends who went from girl to girl to girl. Yet he'd begged her to listen to him, to take him back. After a week, she'd finally relented and went to see him, only to find him kissing yet *another* girl.

That was it. She was *done*.

She'd slammed the door shut behind herself and had never spoken to him again. She'd avoided him ever since, ignoring his phone messages and left his letters unopened.

Now she was driving through his town, on the way to a wedding where she would most likely have to look at him with whomever he was dating.

She made a silent vow to be the most law-abiding citizen Moose Creek had ever had.

If only her college roommate, Viv, and her fiancé, Gabe, had chosen a city venue for their wedding. Davina would have felt more comfortable with more escape routes available. The single road leading up to the inn hosting the wedding didn't allow speeds of more than thirty miles per hour. Hard to beat a hasty retreat when you had to dodge potholes and follow the speed limit or risk getting busted by her ex.

Fifteen minutes later, The Loon Lake Inn appeared. The parking lot was already half-full of cars and trucks bearing license plates from several states.

No police vehicle in sight.

Davina blew out a breath she hadn't realized she was holding.

She went inside, registered at the desk, and made small talk with an elderly couple who were in the lobby. They introduced themselves as Agnes and Albert, Gabe's great-aunt and great-uncle, and practically jumped up and down with excitement about the wedding. When Davina told them she was Viv's college roommate—yes, the one that went on to be a doctor—they shook her hand repeatedly. Viv had talked to them about her more than once, said she was an important doctor in the city. Davina tried to explain that chief coroner wasn't all that big a deal—she dealt with dead bodies more than live ones—but they refused to believe her. They were charming and cut, and their welcoming attitude eased the knot of anxiety tying up her insides a little.

By the time she got to her room, she was smiling.

How long had it been since she felt anything but stress and loneliness? Months? Years?

She really needed to get out more. Take a vacation somewhere like Moose Creek where no one knew her.

She settled for a hot shower and a comfortable summer dress to wear to meet up with Viv and Gabe.

A knock on her door had her smiling again. Agnes and Albert weren't the only excited ones, Viv was early.

Davina opened the door, preparing to give her friend a long hug, but it wasn't Viv in the doorway.

It was Drew.

An older Drew than the man she remembered.

This one was wearing a sheriff's uniform and had his hat in his hands. The broad shoulders, long eyelashes, and boyish smile were all the same, though. He looked in as good a shape as he'd been in college.

The impact of seeing him in her doorway, only a couple of feet away, was a blow to her chest. She'd thought the wound long healed, so why did it hurt so much to breathe?

"Hey, Davina," he said, that smile drawing a couple new wrinkles at the corners of his eyes. "I was hoping we could chat."

Chat? He wanted to *chat*?

The last time she'd seen to him—six years, one month, three weeks, and two days ago—he'd been in the arms of a very naked, very wet woman as they'd exited a shower.

She'd waited five entire seconds for him to begin to explain. Five seconds in which she endured the smirk of his naked playmate while he stared at her blankly then said, "Honey, you have no idea how glad I am to see you." No remorse in his expression. No regret.

That one phrase damn near killed her. A spear to her heart. There were so many less painful ways to break up with a girlfriend than having her discover you with another woman *in flagrante delicto*.

Six years ago, she'd been thrown into a pit of despair.

But she wasn't that shy, too-smart-for-her-own-good, naive girl anymore.

Today, the smile on his face pissed her off and lit an unholy fire in her gut.

Davina pulled her arm back and punched him as hard as she could in the nose.

He stumbled back, his hands going to his face. "What the..." He pulled his hands away. A small trickle of blood rolled down to drip off his lip. He wiped at it, stared at the red then looked at her with wide, shocked eyes.

"Chat?" she demanded. "You want to *chat*? How about we talk about what a two-timing asshole you are? Or maybe we could discuss your lousy way of dumping your girlfriend? Huh?"

"You do realize you just assaulted a sheriff?" he asked, his voice incredulous.

She crossed her arms over her chest and grunted. "You're lucky I didn't kick you in the nuts."

"I never cheated on you," he said, a little muffled by the sleeve he was using to stop the bleeding. "I didn't know who that girl was."

"Well, your hand on her ass told a different story."

"She walked into the shower and grabbed me. I couldn't get her out of there without putting my hands someplace."

"So you chose the crack of her butt?"

"My hand slipped!"

"Really?" she said, enough sarcasm dripping off her words to burn a whole through metal. "So did mine."

She slammed the door, engaged the lock, and glared at it. If he knocked again, she wasn't going to be so nice.

***

What the hell just happened?

Drew stared at the closed door like it shielded the secrets of the universe. All he'd wanted was to talk, maybe offer an apology for what happened six years ago and get one in return for Davina not believing him.

Hoping for a fresh start was probably a little more than was realistic, but a punch in the face hadn't been on his radar at all.

Drew pulled his hand away from his nose and looked down at himself. Jeez, he was covered in blood and it was still dripping off his face.

With one last look at Davina's hotel room door, he headed toward the lobby and the nearest exit. Three steps into the lobby, he knew he'd made a mistake. It was full of incoming wedding guests, including an elderly couple, Gabe's aunt and uncle, who'd treated him like he was family too.

Agnes and Albert looked up from their wedding invitation as he walked in.

"Good heavens, Sheriff, sit down before you fall down," Agnes said.

"Agnes, he can look after himself," Albert told her. He took a second look at Drew and grunted. "Or maybe not."

"He's bleeding," she yelled, one decibel below a scream. Agnes pinned her glare on him and said, "Sit."

Drew sat.

Noelle, who was manning the check-in desk, rushed over with a box of tissues and handed him a couple.

Agnes put her hands on her hips and shook her head. "You look like you've bled enough for two men." She turned her glare on the clerk. "What room is that nice lady doctor in?" She snapped her fingers a couple of times. "Davina. Please ask her to come take a look at Sheriff Cavendish's nose."

Drew had to hide his smile behind his shirtsleeve. "Thanks, Agnes." He was happy to milk her interference for all it was worth. "It's still bleeding."

"Did you arrest the idiot who hit you?" Albert asked, looking around. "Did you call for backup?"

Drew winced. There were way too many police and crime dramas on TV these days. "Um, no. I tripped and whacked my face on a doorknob."

Agnes stopped her fussing and Albert stopped looking for someone large enough to have beat Drew up to stare at him with their jaws open for two long seconds.

"A doorknob?" Agnes's voice was high with disbelief.

A commotion near the entrance to the inn caught his attention. A flurry of people were arriving with luggage. Albert backed out of the way, leaving the newcomers with a clear view of Drew in his blood-splattered shirt.

Two women mixed in with the crowd gasped his name and came rushing over. Leanne Mosby and Tammy Strickland were far more dangerous to his peace of mind than any small-time crook. They were both divorcees looking to find a new man to call their own. They'd set their sights on him last year and had managed to become quite a nuisance to him and his whole office. He'd move, but this was his hometown.

Did the two of them have a bet going on as to who would land him?

Leanne was a blonde with manicured fingernails that were long enough that he wondered how she did anything at all without them getting in the way.

Tammy was a brunette who was too skinny for the massive rack she displayed in low-cut, tight shirts that left nothing to the imagination.

Leanne hip-checked Agnes out of the way with a skill that would have made any NHL hockey player proud. She put her hand, and her dazzling sharp nails, on his neck. Tammy scooted around behind him, grabbed his arm, and turned him toward her.

Leanne tightened her grip on his neck while Tammy yanked harder on his arm, both complaining to the other that they were helping him.

At this rate, they were going to cause more damage than the punch to his face.

"This is the medical emergency?" an irate female voice asked.

Davina. Thank God.

"He looks like he's got all the helping hands any man could want and then some," Davina drawled.

Leanne smiled—at least he thought it was supposed to be a smile—and said in a throaty voice, "It's just a little nosebleed. No need for everyone to panic. I'll take the sheriff home and wash his shirt for him."

"My house is closer," Tammy said. "And I have a brand-new washing machine that takes half the time yours does. He should come with me."

Davina started laughing loud enough to draw everyone's attention. And kept on laughing until she was bent over and gasping for air.

***

Davina wouldn't have believed this situation was happening if she hadn't watched it unfold. Drew Cavendish was about to get ripped in half by two desperate and dateless housewives.

The blonde sneered at her. "Laughing at an injured man is despicable."

"I don't know who you are," the brunette said with her nose in the air, "but this isn't funny. Can't you see he's hurt?"

"With nosebleeds," Davina told them, "it almost always looks worse than it is. Besides, I'm the one who hur—"

"Is the doctor," Drew interrupted.

"You two heifers get your hands off the sheriff," Agnes ordered, her eyes flashing with anger. "Neither one of you has the smarts God gave a squirrel."

The two women sputtered, but didn't let go of Drew.

"How dare y—"

"What a rude thing to sa—"

"You're choking him," Davina interrupted, looking at the blonde's hand on his neck. "You might want to let him go before you murder your precious sheriff."

Drew's face had turned a dark red.

Both women released him and stepped back with gasps of worry and incoherent apologies.

Drew coughed and sucked in air with more effort than was strictly necessary.

Drama king.

Agnes took over, flapping her hands at the two women. "Go on now and let a professional deal with the situation. All you two are doing is causing a scene."

Davina had to work to keep the smirk off her face as she came around to look at Drew's nose. She pulled his wrist and bloody sleeve away from his face. Blood dripped slowly.

She grabbed a couple of tissues, put them in his left hand then picked up his right hand and brought it up to the bridge of his nose. "Pinch here. The bleeding should stop in a few minutes."

Drew mumbled something, but it came out garbled.

Before Davina could ask him to repeat it, Agnes clicked her tongue at him. "You sound like you have a mouth full of marbles, Sheriff. Best to stop talking until the worst is over."

Worst what? Two women were fighting over who was going to take him home. Most men would be happy in his situation.

"Poor man." Agnes shook her head. "You work too hard." She turned to Davina and said in a conspiratorial tone, "He doesn't get enough sleep having to deal with criminals and silly geese like those two who were yanking on him like a wishbone."

Drew sighed with exaggerated patience.

Davina bit her lips to prevent smiling. "Oh?"

"Nag him half to death, they do. I'll bet that's why he tripped, too tired to see where he was going."

She had to stifle a snort. Is that what he'd told people? "Perhaps if he just picked one, the rest would leave him alone. Or does he prefer to keep his options open?"

"Oh no, Sheriff Cavendish doesn't date."

That seemed unlikely. "Really? Why not?" She looked him over. It was impossible to miss his mouth watering muscle tone. She shouldn't needle him, but she couldn't help observing in a fake concerned tone, "He seems handsome enough and has a good job."

"You'd think the world was his oyster," Agnes agreed, then leaned closer and said, "For a while there, the townsfolk wondered if he liked men more than women."

Drew choked and coughed until his breathing wasn't much more than wheezing.

Davina smacked him on the back with a couple of gratifying thumps.

"But finally," Agnes continued, "the sheriff told everyone how he'd lost the love of his life to a misunderstanding. He's still pining for her." She shook her head. "Very sad."

"There's always two sides to every story," Davina replied, pulling some wet wipes from her first-aid kit and wiping the blood from Drew's face. "Maybe the woman in question discovered him cheating on her."

His brows came down in rebuke.

She frowned right back at him.

Agnes shook her head. "I can't believe that. I've seen the sheriff turn down every woman in town, including a recent wealthy widow and several attractive younger ladies who would make a good wife for a sheriff. Good girls who are smart, but also want to stay home and raise a family."

Anger overtook Davina as she finished cleaning Drew's face and nose. Too bad she didn't have some steel wool to scrape the blood off with. "He should have taken one of those fine young ladies up on their offer of a warm home with children. Not every woman can provide that. Take me, for example. As a doctor, I work a lot and I'm seldom at home."

"Your work is important." Agnes patted Davina on the arm. "I'm sure there's a man out there who appreciates that."

Davina gave Drew a significant look. She shouldn't have bothered. Drew wasn't interested in her.

"Thank you, but I'm comfortable with my life as it is." She looked Drew in the eyes and said with complete sincerity, "You really shouldn't wait too long to get married to one of those pretty, nice girls chasing you. You deserve a good life."

Drew's eyes widened.

Davina's stomach dropped like a stone. He was going to know she still...cared. What had she just said?

***

Drew watched the color drain from Davina's face and knew she was about to bolt. She'd done it before. He'd watched her run out of a room and he hadn't seen her again for six long years.

Not this time.

This time, she wasn't getting away that easily. She was going to have to convince him she didn't still have feelings for him, and from her last couple of sentences, he had doubts she could do that.

She cared. He might have to remind her how much, but she cared.

Before she could take off running, he wrapped his hand around one of her wrists. "Thank you for your concern." He wanted to sound serious, but his plugged nose made him sound like he had the world's worst cold.

She pulled at her arm, and he let her go. Slowly.

Davina jerked her gaze away from his and smiled at Agnes and Albert, then began backing away. She glanced at him, but didn't stop moving. "If the bleeding doesn't stop in another fifteen minutes, let me know and I'll take another look." She turned and hurried away.

After she was out of sight, Agnes and Albert both looked at Drew. "You're an idiot if you let that woman get away from you again," Agnes said.

Surprise had him staring at the older couple. "How did you know?"

"We're old, not dumb," Albert explained. "You have no idea the chase this gal led me on before we got married."

Agnes gave her husband a saucy grin. "It was worth every second."

"That it was, my darlin.'" Albert patted his wife on the butt. "The good ones always take work," he told Drew. "If she's the right one, she'll appreciate the effort."

"Grovel, you mean?"

"That's only part of it," Albert cautioned with a shake of a finger. "You've also got to show her how much you love her. It's the little things, son, that make the most difference."

"The little things aren't really all that little to a woman," Agnes added. "Every morning Albert brings me a cup of coffee before I get out of bed. He's been doing it every day since the day we got married."

"When our kids came along," Albert said with a faraway look on his face, "I started doing the dishes every evening after dinner to give Agnes a break. It turned out to have an unexpected consequence."

A blush brought a rosy glow to Agnes's face. "Ain't nothing sexier than a man doing dishes."

There was a mental image he didn't need in his head.

"I think I've got it." Drew got to his feet. "I have some plans to make."

Albert winked. "Go get her, Sheriff."

"I will." Drew strode over to the registration desk. First, he needed a room at the inn.

***

The ice had melted in Davina's Long Island Iced Tea. She took a sip and made a face at the watered-down flavor. She didn't know why she was still here, at the inn's bar surrounded by drunk women, watching those same women consume free drink after free drink.

"Okay, who died?" Viv asked her with narrowed eyes as she sat on the bar stool next to Davina. Viv's friend Margot sat on the stool on the other side. "You look so depressed you're bringing me down with you."

Davina sighed. "I ran into Drew today."

"Oh yeah, Aunt Agnes said you helped him with a bloody nose. That surprised me. I thought you said you wouldn't help him unless he was at death's door."

Davina sipped a little bit more of her watered-down drink. "Yeah, well, I'm the one who gave him the bloody nose."

Viv and Margot stared at her for a second, then burst out laughing.

"Really?" Viv asked.

Davina nodded. "I opened my hotel room door and there he was, asking if we could talk. I got so mad I punched him in the face."

Viv laughed hard enough that she fell off her bar stool. It took her a minute to get up off the floor and make it back to her seat, but once she did she ordered a round of shots. "This we have to celebrate. I'd have paid money to see it."

"He was surprised." She'd surprised herself, too.

"I'll bet."

The bartender placed the shots in front of them and Viv, Margot, and Davina tossed them back.

"You know, he really hasn't dated. He tried, but his heart was never in it." Viv looked at her with an arched eyebrow. "I wonder where it was?" Before Davina could come up with a response, Viv continued with a far easier question. "Then what happened?"

"He went out to the lobby where he ran into Gabe's great-aunt and great-uncle."

"Agnes and Albert?" Viv asked. "They're everywhere. The worst gossips in the family."

"She sent for me to take a look at his nose. When I got there, two women were arguing about who was going to take him home to clean him up and wash his clothes. Agnes didn't seem too thrilled about that idea and said a few choice words to them." Davina smiled at the memory of the expressions on the two women's faces. "Honestly, I couldn't stop myself from laughing."

"Agnes has a sharp tongue," Viv agreed. "I think that calls for another shot." She signaled for another round then said to Davina, "Not sure why she asked for you right off. She's a retired nurse."

"She is?" Agnes had looked completely clueless. "She didn't say anything or try to help Drew." Gossip? Ha. Instigator was more like it.

The bartender delivered the drinks, and they tossed them back.

Viv carried on with her assessment of her soon-to-be aunt, "She likes to play matchmaker. Ten bucks says she saw an opportunity to put you and Drew together and took it."

"He told her about me?" It came out as a squeak, but she couldn't help it. She'd almost choked on her drink.

"Nope. Drew never told anyone who the long-lost love of his life is. Just that he lost her because he was stupid. Agnes is good at that shit."

Davina snorted. "At least he got the stupid part right."

Viv giggled. "That calls for another shot."

Davina lost count of the shots after four. There might have been two more after that, or maybe it was three. She didn't care. She was drunk and damned if it didn't feel good to not care about anything.

Drew could play with all the housewives he wanted. No skin off her nose.

Nose. Davina snorted at the thought. She'd punched his hard enough to make it bleed and she was proud of herself.

He'd had that coming for a long time.

"Okay," she said to Viv and abandoning her bar stool. "I'm going to bed, though after all these shots, I may be going to the bathroom first."

"Are you okay to get to your room?" Viv asked, blinking at her as if a few extra flaps of her eyelashes might clear up her vision.

Davina smiled brightly. "Yup." And trundled off.

She managed to get her hotel room door open after a few tries, but stopped after a step or two inside. Whose flowers were those?

She checked the door number. Yep, this was her room. She glanced at the huge bouquet of roses on the dresser. Where the hell had those come from?

She walked over unsteadily and managed to grab the card without knocking the whole thing over.

Thanks, Drew.

Thanks? For what? A nosebleed? What did he want next time, black eyes?

Next to the flowers was a box of fancy chocolates.

What the hell was wrong with him that he gave her flowers and chocolates after she assaulted him?

Idiot.

Davina grabbed the flowers and chocolates and weaved her way out her door and to the hotel room Drew had written on the card. She was not going to have these stupid things in her room where she could see them and eventually feel guilty enough to thank him for them.

Damn him. She already felt guilty.

She found his room and knocked hard on the door.

It opened to reveal a woman in purple lingerie. One of the two who had fought over Drew in the lobby. Tammy?

"Oh, it's you," the woman said, losing her simpering, seductive expression. "What do you want?"

"I'm surprised to see you. Didn't Agnes send you home?" Davina asked with smirk.

Tammy smiled in the fake plastic way of a used-car salesman. "Sheriff Cavendish invited me over."

Davina glanced over the bimbo's shoulder, but didn't see Drew anywhere.

Bullshit.

Then again...

"These must belong to you, then." Davina held out the box of chocolates. As soon as Tammy took them, Davina tossed the entire contents of the vase—flowers, water, and all—in the other woman's face. "And these. Enjoy."

Tammy screeched, but Davina turned and left before she laughed in the other woman's face. Besides, there was nothing for her in Drew's room except more disappointment and another woman waiting for him to return.

Where the hell was he, anyway?

Davina paused in the hallway, then decided on a slightly different direction. Back to the inn's bar.

It was busy with locals, wedding guests, and, yes, the groom's party had arrived with Drew in the middle of the pack, a beer bottle dangling from his fingers. How dare the rat look relaxed and happy?

She stomped over to him, shoving a couple of guys out of the way even though they tried to offer her a drink. "There you are," she said.

He looked up and smiled like he really was happy to see her. "Hey, Davina, would you like to join us?"

Chat, join—he was all about the casual, the surface. She needed a man who could handle the dark parts of her, as well as the light. "Join you...you jerk. No, thanks."

His smile fizzled out and he frowned. "What did I do now?"

She thrust a finger under his nose and shook it at him. "How dare you give me flowers and candy, then invite another woman for a private party in your hotel room? Have you no shame?"

His body jerked like she'd shocked him. "Say what?"

"You heard me, you two-timing jack...jack...o'-lantern."

"I think you mean jackass," Gabe corrected helpfully.

"Yeah." Davina pointed at Gabe. "That."

"Drew sent you flowers?" Gabe asked with great interest.

Drew covered his face with one hand. "Here we go."

"Yeah, but..." Davina wobbled for a moment before she smiled brightly and rediscovered her equilibrium. "I gave them to the woman in his room."

His hand dropped into his lap. "There's really a woman in my room?"

"Yup. Tossed the flowers and water all over her face and fancy negligee." She snickered. "You'd better get back there before there's a noise complaint from your neighbors. She was screeching like the dead when I left."

"I didn't invite anyone to my room," Drew protested.

"The card you left with the flowers sure seemed like an invite to me," Davina said.

Drew's mouth opened and closed a couple of times before he sputtered, "Yeah, *you*, not anyone else."

"How did she get into your room, then?"

Drew shrugged. "I don't know."

She rolled her eyes. "Again with the *oh, poor me, I don't know how that naked woman got into my room or shower*."

"That was six years ago." Drew threw his hands in the air. "And I didn't invite that one, either."

"You're such a creek." Davina had to blink to keep the world from spinning.

"I think you mean creep," Gabe offered in between chuckles.

"Yeah. That." The room really was going around fast. So was her stomach. "I should have known better than to believe a hot guy like you was really interested in me for more than sex two or three times a day."

Gabe's mouth dropped open. "Two or three...*every* day?"

Davina sniffed. "It wasn't my fault I had so much studying to do. I was trying to get into medical school."

Gabe turned an envious expression on Drew. "Dude, teach me."

Drew groaned. "Someone fucking shoot me."

His words seemed to come from a long distance away. The light in the room dimmed, turning all the people in the bar into indistinct shadows and ghosts.

Gravity stopped working about the same time all the lights went out.

***

Drew managed to catch Davina before her head hit the side of the table.

Next to him, Gabe lost his battle with keeping his laughter in. "Wow, I have never seen her this drunk before."

"Me neither." He'd have to watch her closely to make sure she didn't throw up while she was still out.

Gabe punched him on the shoulder. "You dog. Every day? Holy shit, man, what the hell kind of pills were you popping back in college and why didn't you share?"

"I didn't need any damn pills. Davina is fucking gorgeous. I couldn't keep my hands off her." He still couldn't.

"So, what's with the women getting into your room?"

"I don't know." He looked down into the face of the woman he'd never been able to get out of his system or his heart. "But I'm going to find out." He stood and hoisted her over his shoulder. "Catch you later."

Gabe shook his head. "I can't wait to hear how this goes down. Talk to you tomorrow."

Drew got halfway back to his room before Davina woke up.

"Hey," she said in a slurred voice. "What's going on?"

Drew decided answering her would be more dangerous than keeping his mouth shut, at least until they got to his room.

"Drew, put me down."

He didn't answer, just hurried along a little faster.

"I know it's you. I'd know your pert, muscled ass anywhere."

Keeping his mouth closed wasn't helping. "Huh, we'll discuss that later, after we've had a little chat."

She wiggled and kicked. "Put me down, you Neanderthal."

He kept his tone even. "Nope, you're drunk."

It was a full two seconds before she said, "But I'm not driving. You can't arrest me for drunk walking."

"I'm not arresting you. I'm trying to figure out what the hell is going on, and until I do," he lowered his voice into what his deputies called his all-business tone, "you're not leaving my sight."

She was silent for all of two seconds. "I demand private time to pee."

God save him from drunk women. "You're going to hate yourself tomorrow morning."

"Ha, I already do." She sniffed again. Was she crying? Before he could ask, she ordered in an imperious tone, "Put me down you unfaithful asshole."

Since they'd arrived at his room, and the door was open, he did as he was told. Once Davina was on her feet, he slowly let her shoulders go.

She stumbled into the room and almost tripped over the housekeeping lady who was picking up the last of the flowers on the carpet.

"Well," Drew said, "at least you got the part about throwing the flowers on someone right."

"I didn't throw them on her," Davina said, pointing at the housekeeper.

"I'm sorry, sir," the lady said. "Your wife is in the shower."

"Wife?" Davina asked.

"Wife?" Drew repeated. "I'm not married."

"That's who she said she was," the housekeeper said, horrified. "Earlier when I let her in. She said she'd forgotten her room key."

Davina looked down her nose at him. A feat since he was taller than her by a foot. "You have a big problem with women."

"Only one?"

She rolled her eyes. "I want to go back to my room."

Drew couldn't think of a better idea. He grabbed her hand. "Let's go, twinkle toes."

She shook him loose. "You can stay in your own room."

"No, thanks. It comes with an accessory I really don't want."

"Ha. Funny." She started off down the hall.

Drew had to keep her from falling on her face only twice.

When they reached her room, she tried unsuccessfully to get the keycard into the slot on the door lock several times before Drew took it from her and opened it.

"Thanks," she told him. "You can go now."

As if. "You don't look so good. I think I'll stay to make sure you're okay."

"I'm fine," she said, waving her hands at him. "All I need to do is throw up a few times, and I'll be awesome."

"When are you planning on doing that?" She was almost green enough to pass for a frog.

"Is now too soon?" she asked, covering her mouth with one hand.

Drew grabbed her and rushed her into the bathroom just in time for her to puke in the toilet. He gave her a few minutes to retch without him hovering over her, then wet a washcloth with warm water and wiped her face with it. "Better?"

"Not really," she said as she laid her head on the side of the porcelain bowl. "Tired."

"You going to throw up some more?"

"No..." Her voice tapered off into a sigh.

Drew picked her up and laid her on the bed. He took off her shoes, her pants, and top and tucked her under the covers. He tried really hard not to look, but couldn't help notice that she'd only gotten more gorgeous since he'd last seen her. There was a maturity to her muscle tone that was sexy in a way that caught him by the testicles and didn't let go.

He made himself take a step back and put her room key in his pocket. He was going to figure out who had invited herself into his room and make sure they never did it again. Then he was going to come back.

He wasn't going to let Davina run away this time.

***

Davina was going to smash the old-fashioned hotel telephone ringing three inches from her head into tiny, tiny bits. The sound amplified her headache into an earthquake. She reached out blindly, fumbling around until she found the receiver then yanked it over to her face.

"Hello," she croaked.

"Dr. Hobbs, this is the front desk. We have a hotel guest who's experiencing chest pain. He's refused to go to a hospital, but another guest has convinced him to let you look at him. Would you mind?"

Any other day she would have been happy to. Today, even her hair hurt. How much had she drank last night? "Where is he?"

"Here in the lobby."

"I'll be there in a few minutes." She hung up the phone, rolled over, and came face-to-face with Drew.

She sucked in a breath so fast it cut her throat to ribbons. "*Holy shit.*"

"Who was that?" he asked.

"What the hell are you doing in my bed?" Had she drank enough to invite him to her room? Wait. She lifted the covers to check herself. She was in her underwear and alone under the covers. He was fully clothed and appeared to have slept on top of the covers.

"You were pretty unstable on your feet last night, so I carried you back here. Unfortunately, that was when the alcohol caught up to you and you started throwing up. You passed out in the bathroom, so I cleaned you up a little and tucked you into bed."

"And you invited yourself, too?" It came out a screech.

"No, I was scared you might vomit while you were out cold, so I made the decision to stay. How's your hangover?" His tone was concerned, solicitous, even kind.

She narrowed her eyes. "I hate you."

"That bad, huh?"

"Get out of my room."

"I didn't invite Tammy to my room last night."

Memory flooded in—the flowers and chocolate she'd decided to return to him, only to find the stacked brunette waiting for Drew in a flimsy lace outfit that didn't cover anything. And what she'd done about it.

Davina laughed. "I threw the flowers on her."

"Yeah." He smiled. "I wish I had been there to see it." He rolled off the bed and onto his feet. "If this keeps up, I'm going to charge her with harassment."

Davina couldn't tell if he was joking or not. "Yeah, whatever. I've got to go. Someone might be having a heart attack in the lobby." She swung her feet to the floor and levered herself to her feet.

Drew's eyebrows rose even as his eyes traveled her body. "They call for an ambulance?"

"Hey, I'm up here," she said, pointing at her face.

He didn't look the least bit sorry as he met her gaze. He raised his eyebrows.

"No. Whoever it is, they're refusing to go."

He glanced at her breasts. "You going looking like that?"

God, he was such a guy. She shook her head and went into the bathroom. It didn't take long to use the toilet, brush her teeth, and stick her head in the sink to get her hair wet. When she came out Drew was gone.

About time. Waking up next to him had been a shock. For a moment she'd been taken back in time to those mornings when she woke next to him while they were dating. She'd kiss him awake and make long, slow love, the pleasure exquisite.

Loss twisted her stomach into a tight, painful knot.

Those days were over.

Davina got dressed, grabbed the first-aid kit she always traveled with, and made her way to the lobby.

Drew was already there, asking people to move back.

He looked up and saw her. "Please, folks, the doctor is here. Make a little more room for her to work."

The half dozen people stepped aside, giving her an unobstructed view of an older man sitting in an armchair.

His face was pale and coated in a sheen of sweat. His lips were tinged with blue, almost as if he were wearing lipstick. His breathing sounded labored without a stethoscope and he rubbed his left arm like it hurt.

She approached him, and Drew got the crowd to move back another couple of feet. "Hello, I'm Dr. Hobbs. What's your name, sir?"

He huffed and puffed as he replied, "Richard Zimmerman."

"How long have you been experiencing pain and shortness of breath?"

"About twenty minutes."

She pulled out her stethoscope. "I'm going to listen to your chest, okay?"

"Okay, but I don't want to go to a hospital."

Drew shushed everyone without making any of their audience mad. Now that was talent.

Davina listened to the man's chest. His breathing was very tight, and his heart rate was odd. The beat wasn't steady—there were missing beats, or they were cut short. "Richard, you're going to a hospital. I'm afraid you've got no choice. What you do get to choose is how you're going to go. Either you go in an ambulance or a body bag."

Richard's eyes widened. "It's that bad?"

She nodded. "Yes, it is. So, which do you want?"

He closed his eyes. "Ambulance."

A few feet away, Drew ordered the ambulance with his cell phone. "ETA, ten minutes."

Davina spent the next few minutes asking Richard questions about his medical history, medications, and if he'd experienced these symptoms before.

When the paramedics arrived, she gave them a concise report and suggested treatment.

"Why can't you just order them to give the medication?" Drew asked as one of the paramedics called in to the hospital to get permission to administer the medication Davina suggested.

"I don't have ordering privileges at this hospital, and I'm from out of state." She put her stethoscope away. "It would be like you doing what a sheriff from another state told you to do."

"Huh, I never thought about it that way."

"Plus, I'm a coroner, not an ER doctor. They might have different medication regimens in practice here than I know about or have kept up with."

"Why a coroner?" He scratched his head. "You're good with people. Why would you choose to work with the dead?"

"Because I'm *too much* of a people person."

He scratched his head. "Explain that to me."

"I struggle with maintaining an emotional distance between patients and myself. I have no problem with the dead. Someone has to speak for them, discover if foul play, neglect, or carelessness was involved in their death. I do that. But with living patients, I get too emotionally invested in them. It tore me apart everyday during my residency." She ground to a halt. Why had she told him all that? She cleared her throat and finished with, "My mentor suggested I try the morgue for a while and that's where I discovered my place. I like solving a puzzling death."

"Yeah, you always were a softy at heart," he muttered.

"Has your curiosity been satisfied?" she asked.

"I suppose."

"Good." She turned and walked back to her room.

He followed her. The man was worse than a puppy.

She stopped at the door before unlocking it. "What now?"

"We need to talk."

"No, we don't. I caught you with two different girls. The second one after you convinced me the first one was some kind of prank set up by your teammates." She had to swallow a sob. "And yet, there you were in your bedroom, your tongue down another girl's throat." She turned to look at him but found it difficult to meet his gaze. "Why would you do that?"

She finally made eye contact with him and was rocked by how stark and strained his expression was.

"I'm not going to stop asking," he said, taking a half step closer, crowding her against the door.

Anger straightened her back and she unlocked the door. The room looked the same as when she left it. The bed in disarray, her clothes from the night before thrown on the desk chair.

She turned and put her hands on her hips. "Okay, now's your chance. Talk."

Drew ran a hand threw his hair and looked at the floor for a couple of seconds. Finally, he met her gaze with a rueful one of his own. "I'm sorry." He sighed. "I'm sorry for not making it clear six years ago that the girl in the shower wasn't there on my invitation. I'm sorry for not chasing after you to explain, even though I was buck naked. I'm sorry for being an idiot and kissing another girl to find out if what we had was as good, as special, as I thought."

Every word out of his mouth cut her heart to ribbons all over again. "You weren't sure what we had was special?" She'd known it from the moment they met.

"I admit I was stupid. I had all these friends telling me that one girl was as good as another, and I was so angry that you didn't trust me, I decided they were right."

Every word he said hit her like blows to the body, robbing her of breath, strength, and the ability to think.

"They said I didn't need you, I just needed a warm body, but I found out the hard way that they were wrong."

The knot in her stomach twisted tighter, the pain making her eyes water with tears she refused to shed while he was watching. "That's really dumb."

"Yeah, I knew it the second I kissed that other girl. There was nothing there. Nothing at all. But, when I kissed you, I stepped into paradise." He stared at her with eyes hot with need, his fists clenching and unclenching.

He wanted her.

Her own body responded to the need stamped on him, her heart rate and breathing increasing. "You should go now."

"We're not done." His voice was rough with desire.

"You're forgiven. There," she said, backing up a step. "You've apologized, I've forgiven you, *now* we're done."

One corner of his mouth kicked up and he took a step toward her. "I don't want to go."

She retreated. "You should."

He followed her. "I want to kiss you again."

Her breathing stuttered. "That's not a good idea."

He tilted his head to one side. "Why not? Because you're afraid you'll like it?"

Her back hit the wall next to the bathroom. "Yes." Hell, she'd *love* it.

He put his hands on either side of her face and leaned down until his lips were only a couple of inches from her own. "I've been starving for a taste of your kiss for six years." His breath came in pants and his pupils were huge. "Please."

She opened her mouth to say no, but she hesitated, remembering the pleasure his kisses had given her.

Big mistake. His eyes flared and he covered her lips with his own.

She moaned into his mouth as his tongue tangled with hers. So good. Better, hotter than she remembered. Sensation and need arrowed through her body, making her ache for more than a kiss.

His shoulders were hard with muscle beneath her hands, his legs thicker and harder than before, and when he thrust one thigh between her legs, she found herself rocking against it.

He shifted, his hands on her waist to lift her up on that thigh, while he rubbed his erection against her lower belly.

Her breath caught. His cock was a long, luscious length that had filled her until she'd been afraid he wouldn't fit. The ache between her legs intensified until all she could think about was finding relief.

One of his big hands cupped her breast and she couldn't keep the moan from escaping her throat. His thumb found her nipple and teased it with little touches, as if he were asking permission.

She put her hand over his and pressed his palm against her flesh.

When she let go, he used his index finger and thumb to pinch and roll her nipple, sending a whip of pleasure so intense through her body that she jerked.

Her hands pulled at his shirt as she kissed him frantically, desperate to feel his skin against her own, his hands on her body, his cock inside her.

He pulled back and closed his eyes. "Davina?"

She didn't want questions—she wanted him. Now.

She put her hand on his erection and squeezed.

He lost it.

His hands yanked at her shirt and sent it flying as soon as it cleared her head. Her bra lasted even less time, but he stopped to stare at her breasts. They were fuller now than in college, overfilling his hands as he cupped them with a reverence that had her swallowing down a whimper.

He ducked his head and put his mouth on one nipple and she keened aloud how much she loved it. She wrapped one leg around his and tried to climb him, but he was too tall.

He picked her up and carried her to the bed, not letting her go or pausing in the exquisite attention he was giving to her breast.

Then he switched to the other breast and she couldn't stop the sounds emerging from her throat. Her hands tried to get his pants off, but she was unable to manage anything beyond hanging on to him as he brought her to the edge of orgasm with his mouth and hand on her nipples alone.

He finally moved from her breast to her neck, nipping and sucking his way up to her ear. His hands pulled her pants and panties off, his palms and fingers stroking her butt before dipping between her legs to tease the hypersensitive entrance to her body.

"Drew, please, I need..." She couldn't finish, couldn't get the words out through a throat that was already too tight.

"Are you sure, Dav? God, please be sure because I don't think I'll be able to stop once I get inside you." He rested his forehead against her own and growled, "It's been so fucking long."

"N...now, Drew. *Now.*"

He moved, shifted, the feel of denim replaced by hot skin, and then he was there, the head of his cock pushing inside of her.

She arched her back as he continued his slow penetration, wanting to take all of him.

His body shook as he finally seated himself inside her. "Holy shit." Then he moved and she stopped thinking altogether. There was only the slide of her skin against his, his cock stroking the ache inside her, tightening it into a ball of pleasure, while he muttered unintelligible words in her ear.

He changed his angle slightly and hit a spot inside her that detonated that tight ball of nirvana until it burned through her whole body, setting her on fire.

When she came back to herself, he'd stopped his deep thrusts in favor of little flexes of his pelvis that served to tease all the nerve endings inside her. *How was he doing that?*

He hovered over her, nose to nose. "Look at me."

She opened her eyes. And saw an emotional volcano about to erupt inside the normally calm and controlled man she thought she knew.

He cared. He cared so much it was radiating off him like a nuclear meltdown. It melted the ice fortress she'd erected around her heart all those years ago.

"I'm not letting you run away this time, Davina." His voice was deep and dark. "You can try if you want, but I'm not going to let you get away."

"Drew, I..." Her protest died as he pulled out slowly, so slowly, then thrust back in hard and fast. He did it again and again, until he pushed her into another orgasm.

He followed and as she came down off the high, she realized what he'd been chanting in her ear.

I love you.

Over and over.

***

Holy shit. He blinked a couple of times to be sure he was where he thought he was, and it wasn't all a dream. Balls deep inside Davina, her arms around him and her breasts pillowing his chest.

Her breath shook as she exhaled, her face glowing, her expression shifting from awe to surprise. He leaned down and set his lips against hers gently, giving her room and opportunity to turn away if she wanted. He kept the kiss soft, a tease and a taste of what they'd just done—were still doing.

He sucked on her bottom lip, nipped its ripe flesh and soothed it with his tongue. He pulled back a fraction and she followed, chasing him.

He took over, igniting the kiss into something explosive, shifting so he could pet her breasts the way he knew she liked, making her moan and hook one leg over his.

Just like that he was hard again.

He began moving in her, slowly, savoring every moment of every stroke, wallowing in the swell of pleasure that rose as he picked up the pace and strength of his thrusts.

He'd missed this, *missed her*. The smell of her hair, the satin of her skin, and the music of her sighs and moans as he gave her every bit of himself.

They both came again. This time, when he kissed her slow and easy, he shifted to his side, taking her with him, holding her close.

She clutched at him and he basked in her acceptance. Until he realized she was crying.

"Davina? What's wrong?" He hadn't held back, given her all he had. "Shit, did I hurt you?"

His questions seemed to make her cry harder.

"Davina? Talk to me. Please."

She shook her head, but held on to him like he was her anchor.

Uncertain as to the cause, and unwilling to let her go while she was this upset, he held her close, using his body to warm her, his hands stroking her back.

Finally, after several minutes, she calmed down and pushed against his chest.

He loosened his hold, but only so far. She was going to talk if he had to make love to her a hundred times.

"It never made sense," she mumbled.

"What never made sense?" he asked, tilting her head up so he could see her expression.

"You and me."

"Bullshit."

She gave him a hollow-sounding laugh. "No, really. You're the hottest guy I've ever seen, smart, too, and you wanted me? A geeky girl who likes puzzles, popcorn, and prefers working with the dead. We're not even in the same league."

"You're the one out of my league," he said, kissing her softly. "I'm just a washed-up football player. You're a doctor with more brains than any one person should have and top it all off, you look like a wet dream come to life."

"I do not."

"Do so."

"My nose is too big and my lips are, well, too big, too."

"Your nose is perfect and your lips..." He was hard again just thinking about her lips. "I fantasize about having them around my cock." He thrust one leg between hers and turned them so he was on top again. "Your breasts make my mouth water. Especially since I can make you come just from sucking your nipples."

She stared up at him, her mouth open slightly, her eyes wide. A tear spilled out and trickled down to her ear. "But you'll leave me."

"No," he said, kissing her with all the gentleness he had. "Never. I have *never* stopped loving you."

"How can I believe you? It nearly killed me the last time. I...I loved you so much."

"I swear to you, there's no one else for me. You're my one."

She started to cry again.

"What can I do to convince you?"

Tears flooded her eyes and trailed down her face. "I don't know."

Fuck, she wasn't listening. The second he let her off the bed she was going to retreat, mentally and physically.

"Will you give me a chance to prove it to you? Please?" He kissed her and kissed her. "I only want you."

She calmed finally, and wiped her face. "Okay, but I don't know—"

"I don't know, either," he interrupted. "But I'm going to figure this out." He brought his face down to hers until they were nose to nose. "I will."

He let her up so she could shower and while she was out of sight and earshot for a few minutes, he made a couple of calls.

***

The hotel restaurant was crowded—every table occupied and people waiting for tables to become available—but when she and Drew arrived, the hostess seated them at a table for two in the center of the room.

It seemed like everyone was watching them.

Davina shook her head at her own paranoia and focused on reading the menu. When the waitress came to take their drink order, Drew ordered her favorite red wine, then smiled at her so wide, she knew—*knew*—he was planning something crazy.

Did she want crazy?

She closed her menu then folded her hands in her lap to keep them from shaking. Ever since they'd made love, *twice*, that morning, she'd felt unbalanced. Uncertain. Unsure of what she wanted.

Her breathing grew shallow as all of those unwanted feelings tangled up her lungs.

And now she was going to cry again.

"Hey, gorgeous," Drew said, reaching around the table to take one of her hands in his. "You okay?"

She shook her head, just a little shake, but it was enough to make her want to run away.

"Hmm. I was going to do this later, but maybe I need to do it now." He seemed oddly hesitant.

She met his gaze. "Do what?"

He smiled at her, and keeping hold of her hand, got out of his chair and went to one knee in front of her. His free hand went into a pocket and came out with a small jeweler's box. "I've had this since my grandmother passed away." He flicked it open to reveal a diamond ring. "Will you marry me?"

She stared at the ring—shock having frozen her breathing entirely. "What?"

"I've lived too many years already without you."

She looked into his face and found an open vulnerability there she'd never seen before.

That's when she realized the whole restaurant had gone silent. No voices talking or cutlery clanking as people ate. She glanced around.

Everyone was watching the two of them. Most were smiling, but a few, notably women, weren't.

She looked at Drew again and sucked in a breath. "You...promise?"

His smile lit up the room. "Yes. Do you?"

God, she wanted him. Not just for now, but for always. "Yes."

She was in his arms and the room erupted in cheers and shouts of congratulations.

"So," he asked in a whisper that was hers alone "your room or mine?"

She snorted a laugh. "Mine."

Book Five
Merry Christmas Baby

***

Marine biologist Mattie Clark is moving back to her hometown after the break-up of her marriage, but she doesn't expect to run into her high school crush (literally) only days after returning, or to discover he's not the smooth operator she remembers. Charles Walker survived a horrific fire only to have his whole world fall apart. His fiancé walked out on him, taking his confidence in himself with her. His own family avoids him now, uncomfortable with the scars he carries. He sinks into a depression nothing will cure, except a short, curvy tornado named Mattie Clark. She seems determined to pull him out of the black hole he's been living in, but is this a short term fling or is she willing to stay for the long haul?

***

Merry Christmas Baby

"Juggling would not be a good career move for me," Mattie Clark muttered to herself as she picked up a bag that had fallen to the ground for the third time. Thank god the item inside, a plump new pillow for her mother, was inside its own plastic covering. The paper bag from the store was getting beat up and soggy from falling into the churned snow on the sidewalk.

She walked another block, looking behind her every few steps to be sure she hadn't dropped anything, before dashing into her last stop of the morning. Led Zeppoli, the bakery in Havenport, had the best pastries anywhere. Both her parents were fond of the chocolate chunk cookies. Mattie had promised to bring them a half dozen.

Once purchased, she found room for the cookies in another of her bags and managed to get out through the doorway without losing anything. She took two steps and ran into a wall. At least, it felt like a wall. She bounced backward on the slippery sidewalk and fell smack on her butt.

The wall bent down and spoke to her. "Whoa, are you all right?"

She knew that voice from somewhere. A deep, smooth baritone that resonated in her bones and triggered a memory she sometimes thought was a dream.

"Charles?" she asked tentatively. "Charles Walker?" She stared up at the tall, broad shouldered man who'd extended his hand to her.

At her question, he flinched, but didn't retract his hand. "Yeah?"

She tried to reconcile the man she saw with the one from her memory. Same height, but broader and more muscled. Same hair, but shorter. His face had changed a lot. Scars crisscrossed the left side of his face and neck. Scars that looked melted.

That's right, Charles had gone on after high school to become a fireman. He must have suffered burns on the job.

"Mattie?" he asked staring at her. "Shit, I'm sorry." He caught himself, shook his head and said, "Shoot, I didn't mean to knock you down."

He sounded so concerned she snorted. "Not your fault. You know me, clumsy is my middle name." She took his hand and he hauled her to her feet with ease. His show of strength made her catch her breath before she managed to say, "And you can say shit if you want. I occasionally use it myself these days."

A small smile flickered across his face, pulling at the scar near the corner of his mouth. It was gone the next moment, his gaze turning somber with a speed that surprised her. "Damn," he said, running a hand through his hair and looking at all the packages and bags she'd dropped on the wet ground. "Let me give you a hand."

She sighed with exaggerated relief. "That would be awesome, thank you."

They picked everything up, then Charles cleared his throat. "Where to? Have you got a car parked somewhere close by?" He looked up and down the street, his head jerking as if he were anxious about something.

Anxious? *Charles?*

"Nope, I'm walking." She dredged up a smile from somewhere. "My parents are living in Encore Manor, the assisted living apartment complex, now. Dad had a stroke last year and mom has diabetes. They were having trouble keeping up with their medications and the house, so they made the decision to move a few months ago."

Charles didn't look at her, but his tone sounded sincere when he said, "I'm sorry to hear that."

"It's okay. They like living at the manor. They play card games every afternoon with their friends, and they don't have to cook or clean their apartment themselves anymore." She glanced at him.

He was still staring at the sidewalk and not looking at her at all. "So, you're in town for Christmas?"

"Yes and no. I'm back to stay."

His head jerked up and wide eyes stared into hers for a moment. "That's...good."

Awkward was what this was, but it shouldn't have been. Where was the confident, cool and composed man she remembered? "How are your folks?" she asked instead.

"Fine." He seemed to relax a little. "They're still living at home, but dad is consulting now part time. Mom took up water color painting and my old bedroom is her studio."

"I guess neither one of us can ever really go home."

"Nope." He glanced around the sidewalk then stared at it like it was a priceless piece of art. "Got everything?"

She did one last check. "I think so."

He turned, again without looking at her, and led the way to the Manor at a walk she was going to have to trot to keep up with.

"Charles?" she asked, a little breathless. "Could you slow down a bit?"

He glanced back at her, meeting her gaze for only a moment, before apologizing and slowing down, "Sorry."

They walked side by side for almost an entire block before she thought of anything intelligent to say. "Are you off today?"

An expression of anger flashed across his face before he could smooth it away, and it shocked her. This was not the carefree Charles from high school.

"I'm not working," he said, the words clipped. "On disability."

"Oh, I'm sorry." She mentally kicked herself a few times. Something terrible had happened to him to change him so much.

He didn't respond, but he sped back up to his original pace.

God, why did all the wrong words keep falling out of her mouth? She was a grown woman, but five minutes after bumping into him, she felt like she was sixteen again. Uncomfortable, clumsy, and self-conscious. Only it was worse, because she was making Charles feel that way too.

That couldn't stand. She owed him. He might not remember defending her from two of his drunk friends the night before they all left for college, but she did.

How was she going to fix this?

"I'm a moron," she said, coming to a stop.

He stopped too. "What?"

"An insensitive, inept, dope."

"Uh?" He looked right at her. Really looked.

People said the truth couldn't set you free anymore. *Ha.* "I didn't mean to ask the wrong question, yet that's just what I did. Bam. I mean, what responsible adult does that?" She sighed. "It's a wonder I wasn't voted most likely to end up in jail due to a misunderstanding back in high school."

Charles winced. "Um, Mattie, it's okay."

"No, it's not," she said, pinching her lips together. "No one has the right to make you feel uncomfortable with stupid questions, which is exactly what I did."

"It's fine," he said with all the enthusiasm of a five year old getting a flu shot in the arm.

"Fine?" she shut her mouth and examined him. "Oh, I see, you're doing the *calm down the hysterical female so I can get out of this mess talk.*" She couldn't really blame him. Her ex-husband complained about her going off on rants all the time. "No worries, mate," she said in her best Aussie accent, which wasn't very good. "We're almost there so you don't have to put up with me much longer."

This time, she set the brisk pace.

"Who says you're hysterical?" he asked, following closer behind her than she expected.

"That would be my ex-husband who left me for his younger, prettier bimbo as soon as he got his law degree."

"So, you're comparing me to an idiot?" Charles asked in an incredulous tone.

Did she hear humor in his voice?

Did he really call her ex-husband an idiot?

"No, I've had this reaction to my overt honesty, as my boss calls it, before. Many times. Almost all worded the same."

When she didn't say anything else, he asked, "How were they worded?"

"Two words. Shut. Up."

"Well, sorry, I was just asking a question, and you brought it up first."

"No, that's not what I..." She whipped around and looked at him with narrow eyes. There was a hint of a smile on his face, mostly around his eyes. "You, Charles Walker, are a smart ass."

The humor left his face, draining away in an instant. "Not so smart or I wouldn't look like an extra from a horror movie."

"Oh please, you're gorgeous inside and out. Always have been. Besides, everyone makes mistakes," she told him with a snort. "I married a selfish jerk who couldn't give a woman an orgasm on his best day."

Charles, who had been staring at her with his mouth open wide, coughed and choked out a laugh. "Okaaay."

"See? Too much honesty." She started walking again.

"I don't know," he drawled, sounding like the old Charles for the first time. "It works for me."

"Do you know what my ex-husband liked to say?"

"This has to be a trick question," Charles muttered.

"He said I could only make interesting conversation with a fish, and he didn't sign on to be a merman."

Charles was silent a moment, then asked, "What did you say?"

Mattie turned to walk backwards and grin at him. "I said that since he lacked the mental capacity to understand me, I'd rather be married to a fish."

Charles grinned back at her. "I don't suppose you said that in public."

"I said it in court."

"Awesome." He smiled at her for another second or two then dropped everything he was holding to lunge at her.

She squeaked and threw packages in a scattered arc as she grabbed his biceps to save herself from falling, and dragging him with her, on the slippery sidewalk.

He yanked her close, her body plastered to his, and they froze.

"What—?" she began.

"Pole," he said, thrusting his chin at something behind her.

She glanced over and discovered that she was inches from a streetlamp pole. "Oh." She met his gaze. "I should know better than to not watch where I'm going."

He stared at her, his lips only a few inches from hers and whispered, "Gorgeous?" That one word was infused with a thousand questions and a desperate hope she never thought she'd ever hear in his voice.

She wanted to kiss him, to show him that what made him who he was had everything to do with the man inside and not the scars on his face and body. She'd never been this close to him, and it wasn't enough. Not even a bit. "Yeah," she whispered back.

His lips thinned and twisted and he very carefully set her away from him. He bent and, with a deliberateness that hurt to witness, picked up all of her packages and bags. When he finished, standing tall, and his face devoid of expression, he said, "We're almost there."

He didn't believe her.

Her jaw fell open and she watched him walk by her as failure attempted to suck her into a deep dark hole.

He didn't believe her.

She was a woman ridiculed for too much honesty, and he didn't believe her.

Her hands were nearly numb with cold, but suddenly she didn't feel chilly at all. Heat rose from her gut, embers stirred by irritation and insult, and fanned to flames by outrage. She turned with every intention of calling his disbelief into question, but his tense, raised shoulders stopped her.

He expected to be verbally attacked. Fully expected it. Anything she said now would fall on ears that would translate her words into something he was ready to ignore.

She'd be acting just like whoever made him feel inadequate and ugly.

He'd forgotten one thing.

She wasn't stupid. Well, not about this anyway.

"Hey," she called out, her tone light. "Could you slow down to school-zone speed? I'm going to fall on my ass again if I have to run to keep up."

He slowed, but didn't quite glance over his shoulder.

That's right, buddy boy, I'm not taking the bait.

They arrived at the manor without further conversation. Charles had managed to stay a step ahead of her until they reached the front door, when she dashed forward to open it for him. He had all the bags.

They toed off their shoes and she led him to her parent's apartment. After a quick knock, Mattie opened the door and called out, "I'm back."

"Did you find everything, dear?" her mom called out.

"And then some." Did bringing a man to visit count as Christmas shopping?

Her mother came around the corner from the living room and stopped short when she caught sight of Charles. "Hello Charles, this is a lovely surprise." A smile bloomed on her mother's face.

"Hello, Mrs. Clark, how are you?"

"Fine, dear, fine." Her mom was trying not to laugh at the sight Charles made of standing in the tiny entryway dripping in bags and packages. "Why don't you put all that on the table," she suggested, pointing at the two-seater dinette.

Charles got there and managed to divest himself of everything without dropping any of it on the floor.

"Would you like a cup of coffee?" her mom asked him.

"Uh, no, ma'am. I can't stay."

"How about coffee at Led Zeppoli tomorrow?" Mattie asked, brightly.

Charles looked at her like she'd lost her marbles. "Thanks, but, ah, I can't make it."

"Are you sure?"

"Yeah, sorry."

"Well, maybe later in the week then?"

"Sure." He glanced at her mom, then damn near bolted for the door. "Have a good day."

Geez, he really couldn't get out fast enough.

Mattie waited a few seconds before fixing a determined look on her mother. "What the hell happened to Charles Walker?"

Her mom sighed and helped Mattie move all her purchases from the table to the coffee table in the tiny living room. "He was no different than when you kids were in school together until last year."

"A fire went bad?"

"Very bad."

"How extensive are the burns?"

"I think the paper said thirty percent of his body." Her mom shook her head. "He was in the hospital for several weeks. His fiancé left him."

"Fiancé?"

"Do you remember Jessica Brewster?"

She nodded. "He dated her in school. Popular and pretty. I thought they got married years ago."

"No, engaged for a long time. Until the fire."

"How could she dump him after all that time together, when he needed her most?" Mattie demanded of no one in particular.

"I don't know," her mom replied, "But I do know he's hurting. He hardly ever comes out of his house anymore, and avoids everyone."

"That isn't right.

"Life is hard sometimes, dear."

"I know, but people don't have to make it worse."

Her mother regarded her with wise eyes and a knowing smile. "Have you met any of your new neighbors yet?"

Mattie gave her mother a suspicious look. "No, I don't get the keys until tomorrow. Why?"

"Charles is one of them."

"Is he?" Wasn't that interesting? "You said he's something of a hermit?"

"Yes."

"What would he have been doing over by the bakery?"

Her mother's smile turned into a grin. "Maybe he likes sweets?"

"I have one more errand to run, mom," Mattie said as she put her coat back on. "I'll be back a little later."

"Good luck."

Mattie retraced her path back to the bakery and went inside. When she told the barista she wanted to thank the man who helped carry her packages home, she discovered he had a particular fondness for bear claws. A large cinnamon confection with chocolate chips.

She bought two.

As she was about to leave, she noticed a poster on the window of the shop advertising a book signing the next day at the bookstore in town.

Perfect.

It took her about ten minutes to walk to the home she'd bought the previous week. It was on a quiet street and was bigger than she needed.

Despite her ex-husband's philandering ways, she hoped she wouldn't have to live in it alone.

The house next to it had a yard that was immaculate. Even the snow in the front yard had been groomed with a rake to say Merry Christmas.

Mattie walked up to the front door and knocked. After several seconds of waiting, she knocked again.

Finally, the door opened to reveal Charles staring at her with a frown. "What are you doing here?"

"I wanted to thank you for your help." She held out the bag from the bakery.

He took it like he expected something dangerous to jump out of the bag, looked inside then frowned at her some more. "You didn't have to do this."

"You didn't have to help me either."

"Look—" he began in an almost angry tone.

"Would you go to the book signing at the bookstore with me tomorrow?" she blurted out in a rush.

She wanted to smack herself with the palm of her hand. Could she have sounded more desperate?

He blinked.

She wasn't sure what surprised him most. Her talking so fast or the mega-watt smile she was using to cover up her embarrassment.

"The store owner is holding signed copies for me, but thanks," he said.

She half expected him to shut the door in her face, but he didn't.

Instead, he asked hesitantly, "Did you say you were moving back here?"

He remembered. She couldn't help the mega-watt smile that bloomed on her face. "Yup."

He darted a glance at her. "Why? I thought you were working for one of those whale conservation organizations. You're a marine biologist, right?"

"Yeah, and I was, more or less, living out of a suitcase for the last couple of years, but the World Marine Conservation Organization offered me a position here on the east coast that won't require much travel. You have no idea how excited I am to have someplace to call home again."

"Well," he said, shifting his weight to lean on the door frame. "Welcome back."

"Thanks."

"When does the big move happen?"

"I get the keys tomorrow."

He chuckled, "Nice Christmas present to yourself."

Wow, he was finally starting to sound the old Charles. "I think so."

"What part of town is your place in?"

Funny you should ask... "Right next door." She pointed at the vacant house next to his, then, before he could say anything, she stepped back and waved. "See you later."

Mattie walked briskly down the sidewalk and managed to keep from turning to look over her shoulder.

The shock on his face—priceless.

The book signing the next day was a zoo. The book store was packed, and Mattie ran into a few of her high school class mates. When she offered to take Charles's signed books to him, the owner of the store seemed pleased to have someone offer to do it.

Or, maybe the older lady was matchmaking.

The day started with a light dusting of snow, but by the time the book signing was underway, the snow was coming down a lot harder. It only got worse as the day wore on.

By the time Mattie was walking back to her new place, with Charles's books in the same bag as her own, the wind and snow had picked up until it was nothing less than a blizzard.

Her new home was dry and warm, but empty. She'd set up camp, literally, in the master bedroom with a blow up mattress and sleeping bag.

She had to purchase almost everything from pots and pans to furniture. She wasn't looking forward to that chore. Her mother would probably love to help, but she didn't have the energy she used to and Mattie didn't want to wear her out.

Thankfully, she had another job she'd much rather do, delivering Charles' books.

She marched over to Charles's place. Well, she tried. It was hard to march through a whiteout.

She knocked on the door, and this time Charles answered it right away.

"What are you doing out in this mess?" he demanded, gesturing at the blanket of snow falling steadily.

"I got my keys this morning, so I'm moved in to my new house. I stopped at the book signing and picked up your books for you."

He looked at the house next door dubiously. "I think I would have noticed a moving van."

"I didn't need one, living out of my suitcase, remember? I've got a blow up mattress and a sleeping bag set up though. Tomorrow I'll start looking for furniture."

"A sleeping bag and a blow up mattress?" Charles repeated slowly. "You're kidding, right?"

"Nope."

"Anything to eat over there?"

She winced. "No, not really. I haven't had time to shop. I was going to order pizza."

He stared at her like she was a math problem no one could figure out. "Would you like to come in for coffee and a bowl of soup?"

She hadn't expected him to offer, but wasn't going to look a gift horse in the mouth. "Sure."

He stepped aside and she walked into the house—and left winter behind.

Plants, many flowering, and all appearing at the peak of health, were everywhere she looked. The air smelled of green growing things, the temperature neither too hot nor cool, like walking into a spring afternoon.

"Why doesn't it feel humid in here?" she asked.

"I have an ultra-efficient furnace with a dehumidifier," Charles said. "It keeps the place from becoming a sauna."

"You could make a killing renting out your living room as a rainforest spa."

The chuckle that rumbled through the room dispelled the lingering worry in the back of her head about furniture and food.

She turned to arch a brow at the man who leaned against the entryway wall, but he didn't say anything. "All you'd have to do is add a couple of fish tanks and this would be nirvana."

"Trust you to want fish among my plants."

"Tank water is perfect for plants, contains natural fertilizer from fish poop."

Charles laughed out loud. "Fish poop, huh? You learn that in college?"

"Nope, from an old fisherman I worked for during the summer between my first and second years in college." She smiled. "He was this crusty old bugger who swore every third word, but I've never laughed, or worked, so hard as that summer." She cocked her head. "What did you do that summer?"

"I worked for Jessica's dad."

And just like that, all the mirth was gone. He strode past her and into the kitchen, which looked like it belonged in a photo shoot from an interior decorating magazine.

"Did you decorate this yourself?" she asked hesitantly.

"Yeah," he said messing around with a professional looking espresso machine. "Jessica had it all in black and white, but I prefer earth tones."

"I," she announced. "Am suffering from foot in mouth disease." She sighed. "Shall we just get her name out there and stomp on it?" Mattie lifted a foot. "Jessica." She stomped her foot down then twisted for good measure. "There, she's stepped on."

Charles glanced at her, but didn't say anything until he turned around with a cup of steaming liquid. He set the cup in front of her on the island in the middle of the space.

"Ooh, this is smooth," she said. "Thank you."

Charles leaned against the island and crossed his arms. "Don't be too hard on Jessica. It was tough for her too after the fire."

Mattie put her coffee down very carefully on the island then said with firm precision, "Bullshit."

Both Charles's eyebrows went up.

"She left you after the fire where you were burned, am I correct?"

A slight tightening of his lips was the only sign the question bothered him at all. "Yeah."

"Did she get hurt in the fire?"

"No."

"Did anything change for her after the fire?"

This answer was a little slower in coming. "No."

"So, you were injured, burned and had to stay in a hospital for an extended period, right?"

"Yeah. I had several surgeries, but this," he pointed at himself. "Was the best they could do."

Wait. *Did he really say that?*

"The best they could do?" she repeated, her voice rising with every word. "Are those your words or Jessica's?"

He just stared at her.

"What the hell kind of Kool aide did Jessica slip into your coffee machine over there?"

He opened his mouth to say something, but she cut him off.

"Do not defend that shallow guppy. She always was all about the flashy exterior. Never had a bad thing happen to her, but I expected more from her than that bullshit." She fixed her narrowed gaze on him. "There is nothing wrong with you."

"Lie." He barked out, then flinched at his own voice.

"No lie," she said marching over to him and poking him in the chest with an index finger. "There is nothing wrong with everything that matters, the stuff in here," she tapped his chest then his head. "So, the outside got a little dented up, so what?"

He snorted. "Not a whole lot of people rushing to tell me all that." He walked away a few steps, then turned back. "My fiancé left me, and her parents patted me on the shoulder telling me that there was still a lot from life I could expect. My injuries shouldn't be a barrier to success, but Jessica, her life was going in another direction."

They hadn't. No one could be that cruel, but, she could see from his face that they had. "And you believed that sanctimonious shit?"

He shrugged and paced back and forth again. "I guess I never had anything bad happen to me until then either."

She didn't believe it, not for a second. "Charles, you're a firefighter. You had to have seen awful things before."

"Yeah, but it was always someone else suffering, not me." He paced back and forth again. "I never really thought about how hard it is for someone to adjust to life after..." his voice trailed off. "After."

Mattie put her hands on her hips. He needed an attitude adjustment. "You look like you're moving okay."

Charles stopped moving to stare at her. A moment later he pulled the t-shirt he wore over his head and dropped it on the floor.

She gasped and walked toward him.

The left side of his torso was covered in burns, some worse than others, given the depth of the scars. His left arm looked as if something large and feral had taken a bite out of it. The resulting scar tissue, tight and twisted, restricted his range of motion.

"Not so okay after all is it?" His tone was belligerent.

He thought she was going to flinch, to walk away like his fiancé.

Nope.

She took the final two steps to reach him then put her hand on his shoulder. She slid her palm down his arm slowly, learning the contour and shape of him. She moved her hand to his torso and skated her palm over the burns there too.

"You see ugliness, I see bravery. You see disability, I see a man who has more than one skill, more than one passion." She glanced around. "Look at your home. You've turned it into an oasis. A place of beauty and food for the soul." She looked into his face and willed him to see what she saw. "You could do this for other people."

He blinked and said, "You think I should become an interior decorator?"

She rolled her eyes. He was such a guy. "Well, when you put that way it does sound a little odd for a manly man like you."

He gave her a gotcha look. "Now who's full of shit?"

"I'm not kidding,"

"You should be." His voice rose in pitch as he talked. "You should be looking at a guy who's in your league with those big eyes of yours, not me." His anger was as palpable as a whip lashing her.

"You don't get to tell me who I like looking at and who I don't," she said stepping up to poke him in the chest again. "You're ten times better looking than my ex-husband." Charles shook his head, but she wasn't done. "You see scars on your body, but I don't. I see marks of courage, of service. I see a man I'd boink if given any encouragement at all."

He smiled, but it was a brittle thing, and said, "Consider it given."

She snorted. "Right. You don't really mean it. I'm the clumsy, curvy girl remember. The only times you spoke to me in high school were when no one else was looking."

"That's because I was sure you weren't interested in a jock who didn't have half your brains."

"Excuse me?" He'd been on the honor roll. "I'm no smarter than you."

"You always knew what you wanted to do with your life, and you went after it no matter what. My parents wanted *me* to break into professional sports. I *didn't*." He stopped talking to take in several deep breaths.

"Football, wasn't it?" she asked hesitantly.

"Yeah. I had the ability," he said with a harsh edge to the words. "But not the love of the game. I wanted to be a firefighter. It's the only job I ever wanted. It took the scouts passing over me in college for my family to let that dream go."

"I'm sorry," she said in a soft tone. "I didn't know."

"Your parents supported you one hundred percent, didn't they?"

"Yes, but they're academic types. They wouldn't know a football from a softball."

"There were times when I wanted to be a member of your family so bad," he muttered.

"You're a good man, Charles," she told him with quiet conviction. "Always have been."

He shook his head.

"Hey. You saved me from something pretty awful that last night before we all left for college. Remember?" She'd never forget. Two of his buddies, drunk and rowdy, had cornered her against a fence a block from her house. They'd said disgusting things, tried to touch her, but

Charles had arrived with a shout and pushed both of them away from her and told her to run.

So, she *ran*.

He looked at her and the heat in that gaze should have left burns on her skin. "Don't go making me out to be some rescuing angel. Not then and not now. You've got killer curves any man would love to get his hands and mouth on." He stepped toward her and she automatically stepped back. He kept coming until he had her crowded against the refrigerator door. "You're wrong about what I want, because I've wanted you from ninth grade until doomsday." He put his hands, one scarred the other not, on either side of her head. "So, are you ready to admit that you're just trying to make me feel better?"

He did not just say what she thought he said.

"You've wanted me since..." her voice died.

"Ninth grade." He leaned down and put his mouth next to her ear, sending a shiver down her back that had nothing to do with the weather outside. "You used to sit in front of me in math class." His voice rumbled out of his chest to tease her neck. "You talked to the numbers while you worked. Sometimes you gave them shit."

"Numbers don't like me," she whispered, then swallowed hard. "My husband told me I was a cold fish."

Charles stroked her cheek with his left hand. "You don't feel cold to me."

"You really...like me?"

"Do you really like me?"

"Yes," she said.

"Yes," he said.

She waited for him to kiss her, he was only an inch or two away, but he didn't. He hovered slightly above her, waiting.

He wanted her to make the first move.

She wanted to remember this moment for a very long time.

Letting out a breath, she rose, her lips capturing his bottom lip in a slow slide. He groaned, so she did it again, then rose a tiny bit more to kiss him fully. It seemed to take forever and almost no time at all.

She pulled back to gauge his reaction.

His eyes watched her with ferocious intent, his pupils dilated. As she looked at him and smiled, he growled.

That was all the warning she got.

His mouth took hers in a sensual tsunami that rolled over her in an unstoppable wave. His hands slid, one behind her back, the other behind her head and jerked her up against him.

She wrapped her arms around his neck and encountered the burns on the left side of his neck and shoulder.

He lifted his mouth, pressed his erection against her belly and all but snarled, "If you don't want me, for *real* want me, you need to tell me to back the fuck off right now."

What was he saying? It made no sense. "Why would I do that? I've wanted you since forever." She kissed his neck.

He shuttered and buried his face under the curve of her jaw.

"Charles?"

He clutched her tighter.

Hmm, if she wanted some smexy time, she'd better give him a clue. She angled her head, caught his earlobe with her teeth then sucked on it.

He began kissing his way up her neck. "Trying to get my attention?"

"I'm trying to get into your pants." Their lips met, tongues tasting each other. "How am I doing so far?"

"Fucking A." He backed up, bringing her with him, kissing her every step. "But I don't want to do this against my refrigerator."

"Why not?" she asked, laughing. "It looks sturdy enough."

"Not." Kiss. "Sturdy." Kiss. "Enough." Kiss.

"You don't scare me," she said, giving him a Marilyn Monroe smile as he tugged her out of the kitchen, down a short hall and into a large bedroom. "You're turning me on."

"Mattie," he said as he kissed her again. "Shut up."

"You—"

The bed was under her the next moment and Charles was over her, one knee between her thighs, and she stopped thinking altogether.

His hands moulded her breasts, teasing her nipples. He kissed his way down her neck and lower, then wrestled her out of her shirt when it got in the way. He looked down at her, hunger alive on his face. He traced the edge of her bra with one finger then slide his hands around to the back closure and undid it. He tossed the bra over his shoulder and stared at her breasts for a moment. Then he met her gaze, leaned down and sucked one nipple into his mouth, lashing it with his tongue.

Her back bowed under as pleasure whipped through her. "Ohmigod."

"You can just call me Charles," he murmured as he abandoned one nipple to torment the other.

She gasped and laughed at the same time. "Funny." She ran her hands through his hair and down his shoulders until she could rake her nails lightly over his nipples.

Without moving his mouth from her breast, he took her wrists, one in each hand, and pressed them against the bed next to her head.

"Hey," she complained with another gasp as he used his teeth to ramp up the pleasure. "No fair."

"You touch me," he said sliding his mouth lower. "And this is going to be over real quick."

"That just means we get to start all over again."

He looked up at her, his mouth at the waist of her jeans. "How many times are we talking here?"

"Um, I wasn't going to put a number on it." Did he see this as a one night stand? "Are you?"

He let his gaze roam her before returning to her face. "I don't know, maybe ten gazillion." His hands found her breasts again. "These have me ready to come in my pants, so I might have to add a few...trillion."

She had no idea he was this hilarious, but the discovery only made her want him more. "That's *not* where I want you to come."

His gaze brightened with heat and he began opening her jeans, tugging them off along with her underwear, with pulse pounding haste. He stared at her sex, her shaved, smooth, delicate skin and said under his breath, "Holy fuck."

"Stop talking," she ordered. "And take off your clothes."

He stumbled off the bed, working at his own jeans without paying much attention. He seemed unable to look away from her.

She'd never felt sexy until today, until this moment.

He shoved his jeans and underwear down then grabbed a condom from the bedside table, opened the package and rolled it on. Over cock a whole lot bigger than her ex-husband's.

"Wow," she breathed out. "You're...big."

He crawled over the bed to her.

"You're a fucking bombshell." His hands outlined her, starting at her breasts then making their way down to her thighs. "Thank God your ex-husband is an idiot."

If she hadn't already thought Charles was ten thousand times a better man than her ex, that statement would have done it. "We should introduce him to Jessica," Mattie suggested, putting a hand behind Charles's head and tugging him down. "One idiot to another."

He didn't reply except to kiss her, his mouth making love to hers as he made room for himself between her legs. He put his hand on her sex and thrust a finger into her.

"So fucking wet." He groaned, his breathing almost a pant. "I can't wait, I'm right on the edge."

"So am I," she said reaching down and taking him in hand. "Hurry up." She guided him to her and he didn't hesitate to push into her in a long, slow thrust that had both of them groaning.

He panted for a long moment, then pulled out and pushed back in. "Fuck, I'm not going to last long."

"Faster," she begged.

He picked up the pace and the climax that shook her on the third stroke seemed to come out of nowhere.

She cried out and hung on through the intense pleasure, only dimly aware that he followed her into orgasm.

Clarity returned after a minute or two. Charles was kissing her neck and was still buried deep inside her.

"This is an awesome neighborhood," she said. "The people here are so welcoming."

Charles started laughing. He withdrew from her, his whole body shaking with his laughter. He rolled onto his side and pulled her with him, so they were facing each other.

He played with her hair. "I'm not with the welcome to the neighborhood group, but I'm really glad we bumped into each other yesterday."

"Me too." She thought about staying quiet, but decided honesty was her only policy. "I always wanted you, too."

"I was so stupid back in school. I wanted to ask you out, wanted you, but my friends—"

"It was the same for me," she said, cutting him off. "We were both young and a little stupid."

The crooked smile on his face, happy and relaxed, made him look so different than when she'd first seen him yesterday. "Here's to being older and wiser."

Mattie kissed him and sang, "Merry Christmas Baby."

Did you love *Men of Action*? Then you should read *Trapped with the Secret Agent*[1] by Julie Rowe!

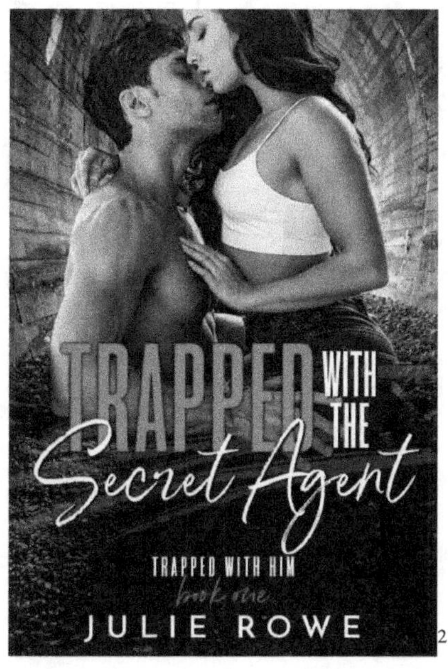

[2]

Terrorists have taken over the American embassy in Koutu, a small Middle Eastern country with huge oil reserves. This is not good news for the Ambassador's claustrophobic personal assistant, Georgia Masters, whose composure is tested when she's locked in a small dark small storage room by the terrorists. Then her worst fear is realized when they throw a man into the storage room with her.

Burned out CIA agent Peter Welis can't believe his bad luck. Terrorists take over the US embassy of a small Middle East country while he's there on a routine visit. Only his cover as a photojournalist saves him from being immediately killed. Then he's locked up in the basement with the Ambassador's claustrophobic secretary. So what if

---

1. https://books2read.com/u/brvzjM

2. https://books2read.com/u/brvzjM

she's bravely trying really hard not to lose her cool. Nothing worse could possibly happen, right? Wrong. After escaping the storage room, he and Georgia discover a crate on the floor covered with Russian printing. It contains a nuclear warhead. Peter is now duty bound to find out the terrorists' true intentions and stop them any way he can.

As they escape the embassy and search for help, hope, and rescue, Georgia struggles not to fall for the secret agent who's the first to tell her he's a bad bet.

Read more at www.julieroweauthor.com.

Also by Julie Rowe

Biological Rapid Response Team
Deadly Strain
Lethal Game
Viral Justice

Sinners Never Die
Sinner's Secret
Sinner's Sacrifice
Sinner's Salvation

Trapped with Him
Trapped with the Secret Agent
Trapped with the Undercover Prince
Trapped with the Covert Ops Soldier
Trapped with the Reclusive Playboy
Trapped with the Ice Station Chief

Standalone

Footprints on my Heart
Men of Action
The War Girls

Watch for more at www.julieroweauthor.com.

About the Author

Julie Rowe's first career as a medical lab technologist in Canada took her to the North West Territories and northern Alberta, where she still resides. She is the author of the Biological Rapid Response Team series, The Outbreak Task Force series, the Trapped with Him series, and the Sinners Never Die series. You can find out more about her books at her website http://www.julieroweauthor.com. You can find her at www.julieroweauthor.com , on Twitter @julieroweauthor or at her Facebook page: www.facebook.com/JulieRoweAuthor

Read more at www.julieroweauthor.com.